ANNABELLE SAMI   ILLUSTRATED BY DANIELA SOSA

Agent Zaiba
INVESTIGATES

THE POISON PLOT

LITTLE TIGER
LONDON

Agent Zaiba
INVESTIGATES

For my nanny, who taught me how to bake and gave me her
wicked sense of humour. Love you x
– AS

To my girl squad and our endless chats
– DS

With special thanks to Speckled Pen

STRIPES PUBLISHING LIMITED
An imprint of the Little Tiger Group
1 Coda Studios, 189 Munster Road,
London SW6 6AW

www.littletiger.co.uk

First published in Great Britain by Stripes Publishing Limited in 2020
Text copyright © Speckled Pen Limited, 2020
Illustrations copyright © Daniela Sosa, 2020

ISBN: 978-1-78895-207-1

1

THE BEST DAY OF THE YEAR

Zaiba stood in front of the huge oak tree in the middle of the village green, gazing up at a poster:

BECKLEY SCHOOL
SUMMER FETE

SATURDAY 2ND JULY   11AM – 5PM

BAKING COMPETITION
(major prize to be won)
FACE PAINTING
SECOND-HAND BOOKS & TOYS
SOAK THE TEACHER
TOMBOLA
RAFFLE
♪ LIVE MUSIC ♩♪

The last, and most important, item on the poster, in extra big, hand-painted lettering read:

TREASURE TRAIL

This was the fifth poster Zaiba had seen today. There had been others on the post box, in the sweet-shop window, tacked to the park gate and even taped to the side of a dustbin lorry. The whole village was going mad for her school's annual summer fete. This was the thirtieth year of the fete and everyone was excited! It had been running even since Zaiba's dad had gone to school – and that was a *long* time ago.

All around the green, tents and stalls were being erected, ready for the crowds to descend. Bunting and posters were strung from every fence and lamppost, filling the school playground with bright colours. Not only was this Zaiba's favourite day of the whole year, today was going to be extra special because she'd been given a huge responsibility... She was in charge of the treasure trail competition! And in true Zaiba fashion, she'd adapted it into a Detective Trail.

"I don't see why I have to go to school on a *Saturday*," Ali grumbled. Clearly this wasn't her younger brother's favourite day of the year.

"But Ali, I thought you were excited about Soak the Teacher?" Zaiba ruffled his long fringe. Ali had been growing out his hair like the members of his favourite boy band, much to their mum's disappointment.

Ali's eyes lit up. "Oh, yeah... My form tutor said he'd be in the stocks at half past four." He rubbed his hands together gleefully.

"Mr Thompson is always up for a laugh," their dad said, striding ahead. "Not sure how he'll feel about a sopping-wet sponge to the face though."

"I'm more excited about Zaiba's detective trail," Jessica said. "This is a big moment for her!"

Jessica was Zaiba's stepmum, and as far as Zaiba was concerned she was the best one in the world. Ali ran on in front of Zaiba and Jessica, holding up his shiny blue camera. Zaiba quickly struck a pose. She had come dressed for detecting in her denim shorts, a sparkling-white T-shirt and running shoes. Fashion didn't really factor in a detective's outfit but Zaiba thought she looked pretty good nonetheless.

"Say cheese!" said Ali, snapping a shot and then inspecting the result. "Hmm, I'll have to turn down the exposure ... Mum's top is too bright!" Ali was in charge of taking photos for the school newspaper – a role he took very seriously. Their dad, Hassan, was so impressed with Ali that he'd even bought him a brand-new digital camera.

"Make sure you get some good photos of my detective trail," Zaiba instructed.

Zaiba wanted to make the treasure trail extra special this year. There were twists and turns, riddles and mysteries to crack – plus a list of likely suspects. She had spent every evening over the past two weeks planning it out. After school, she'd walked the entire circuit of the village green along with Poppy, her best friend. They had carefully mapped out the grounds, looking for special hiding places. Then the two of them had worked out a set of clues in the form of riddles that would point to the locations. Zaiba wanted everyone at school to know how fun and rewarding being a detective could be.

"Why wouldn't anyone want to be a detective?" she'd said to Poppy as they'd stuck ideas on to their mood board.

"I know!" Poppy had agreed, taping on a picture of a magnifying glass. "Think of the accessories!" Poppy loved fashion almost as much as she loved solving crimes.

If Zaiba could get this right, she was certain that her detective trail would make this summer fete special. Of course it wasn't the same as solving a real-life crime but she'd had no luck finding one of those since the case of the missing diamond collar a couple of months ago. It had been so thrilling to track down the runaway dog and its stolen collar! But since then...

Zaiba couldn't help sighing as she stuck on another picture. She'd searched *really* hard for a crime to solve. She'd even called her Aunt Fouzia – the best detective in the whole of Pakistan. Aunt Fouzia had given her some tips about looking for clues. "Look for suspicious behaviour," she'd suggested. "Anyone behaving out of character." Zaiba had done her best. She'd watched the paperboy in case he tried to break into the house – no luck. She'd flipped through most books in the library van to search for sinister handwritten messages – nothing. She'd even volunteered to help at the local five kilometre race to see if anyone tried to cheat, but every runner had won a medal fair and square.

"A crime will arrive when you least expect it," Hassan had reassured her, brushing a hand over Zaiba's hair. In the meantime, she would have to be patient. And for now, the detective trail would help satisfy her detective instincts.

The night before she'd had a video chat with her aunt Fouzia, who was in Pakistan, to discuss the preparations. Her auntie was one of Zaiba's idols, a no-nonsense lady who ran the Snow Leopard Detective Agency in Karachi – one of the top detective agencies in the world! Zaiba had learned so much from her already, and they had gone over every detail of her trail in depth, making sure there would be no mistakes.

"And you've walked the trail through yourself at least three times..." Aunt Fouzia had said over the crackly connection. "We have to uphold our reputation as world-class detectives!"

After Zaiba had solved the mystery of the pedigree pup's missing diamond collar, Aunt Fouzia had asked her niece to set up a branch of the agency in the UK – something Zaiba wasn't taking lightly. She didn't want to let her aunt down!

"I promise, Auntie – you can trust us! Poppy and Ali were my test competitors and we've fixed any problems."

Aunt Fouzia had looked reassured. She knew she could trust Ali and Poppy.

"Perfect! Then I'm sure it will be a success. I wish I could be there to see it." Aunt Fouzia had smiled and Zaiba had felt a pang of sadness. It could be difficult when your family lived far away, but she knew that Aunt Fouzia was needed in Pakistan. "Now I must go, Beti. I'm meeting with the Chief Defence Minister today at the National Bank. I can't tell you why, but they need my expert opinion on a very serious matter..."

Zaiba had gasped and immediately wanted to know *everything*. "Does it have something to do with the Bollywood star whose bank vault was broken into? I read that they stole all of her gold!"

"Let's just say..." Aunt Fouzia had moved closer to the camera, the silk of her sari whispering. "Hers wasn't the only one." Then she had tapped the side of her nose as she always did when something top secret couldn't be mentioned.

Now, as Zaiba walked across the village green, she realized she was smiling from ear to ear. Having such an important auntie certainly had its perks!

It was only mid-morning but the sun was already beating down as parents and children made their way to the school to help set things up. The Victorian building was located at the far end of the village green, tall and hulking against the skyline. The grass was covered in tent poles and canvas, and Zaiba could make out a host of people trying to fit them together.

Running along the other side of the green was the pride and joy of the village – the public gardens, famed for their stunning displays of flowers and the pretty water feature in the centre. It also contained a beautiful rose garden that the school helped to upkeep as part of a community project.

"Come on," Jessica said, squeezing Zaiba's hand. "Let's take the path through the petunias." Zaiba's stepmum was a huge fan of flowers – Hassan never forgot to buy her a bunch every Saturday and he'd learned to grow sweet peas in the back garden to make her happy.

Jessica's smile broadened as they picked their way along the winding path, her top blowing in the breeze. Beneath her arm she carried a big, wooden box as she was in charge of the fete's face-painting stand. Jessica was an art teacher at a local college and loved any excuse to get creative! She had brought along plenty of supplies: multi-coloured paints, a variety of sponges and a brand-new set of glitter.

When the postman had delivered the glitter, Zaiba had held the sparkling tubes up to the light and read the label: **Biodegradable Glitter!**

"Who says you can't care for the planet and have glittery fun!" Jessica had said, packing up her bags.

Now the fresh breeze was making the colourful bunting on the tents flutter and the flowers bob their heads up and down, but when Zaiba looked at her stepmum she was frowning.

"Oh dear," Jessica sighed. "A lot of these rhododendrons have their heads missing. People shouldn't pick the flowers, they're for everyone to enjoy!"

"Rhodo-whats?" Zaiba's dad asked, catching up with them.

"Look!" Jessica pointed to a corner of the garden. Beneath the branches of a weeping willow were clusters of bright pink flowers. But Jessica was right – some of the green stalks were missing their blooms!

"Who would do that?" Zaiba asked. It didn't seem right to cut down flowers that belonged to everyone in the village.

"The florist?" Ali asked.

"Mrs Bailey would never do that!" Jessica said. "She only buys her flowers from the finest flower markets! Isn't that right, Hassan?"

Zaiba saw a flash of guilt pass over her father's face. She knew that sometimes he forgot to stop at Mrs Bailey's shop – *The Tilted Tulip* – and had to buy Jessica's flowers from the petrol station on his way home from work. Zaiba had spotted the sticker one time but had promised to keep her dad's secret.

"Yes, that's right—" he began.

"And look!" Zaiba interrupted. "The stalks are all torn. Whoever did this didn't even use scissors!"

Jessica shook her head angrily. "Vandalism! Besides, people should be careful handling rhododendrons."

Hassan took her gently by the shoulders and steered her out of the flower garden before her mood could sour any further. "Come on, everyone. Let's not spoil the day. What's happening over there?"

A cheer floated up from the school gates and Zaiba spotted the balloon modeller arriving, carrying a red balloon giraffe under one arm.

"You're right, Dad!" she cried, running ahead. "There's a school fete waiting for us!"

2
BAKING TIME!

The Shah family hurried through a white picket fence
that marked the end of the public gardens. There was a
small road to cross over to the school, where a banner
strung across the railings read: '**Beckley School Summer
Fete**'. Ali snapped a photo and Zaiba felt a fresh flurry of
excitement!

As they walked over, they passed a couple of kids
playing hopscotch on a grid they'd marked in chalk –
right in the middle of the road! The fact that the roads
around the green would be closed on the day of the
school fair had made it even more exciting to plan the
trail. Zaiba's detectives could run anywhere – as long

as they didn't knock over the badge stall or disturb the animals in the petting zoo!

In the playground, two ladies were helping at the registration tent, where people could sign up for all the activities going on that day. They both had walkie-talkies attached to their belts. Zaiba guessed this was so the fete organizers could stay in contact at all times. She felt a stab of envy – they looked so much more professional than mobile phones! Maybe she could save up for one ... or rather three, as Poppy and Ali would need their own too.

"Come on, Ali!" Hassan jogged ahead, pulling Ali behind him. Zaiba could guess exactly where they were going – to put their names down for the parent-child baking competition! This was the biggest competition at the fete, running since the very first one.

Hassan was absolutely determined that they would win it this year. He'd been up early every morning for the past week, baking cupcakes. Their kitchen had practically turned into a cupcake factory. At first this had been brilliant, but after eating seven cupcakes in a row Zaiba had started to feel decidedly queasy. Even Poppy, who was a massive foodie and *loved* cakes, stopped calling round after a few days. Zaiba never, *ever* thought she'd say this, but there was only so much sugar a person could take! She thought she might turn green if she had to even *think* about baked goods.

"Are you coming?" Jessica said, following after the others. "I want to make sure they don't try to sign up twice. They'd do anything to get inside that baking tent!"

Zaiba shook her head and pointed towards a fold-out table on the other side of the playground. "I want to see how many people are interested in the detective trail."

"OK, sweetie, see you later!" Zaiba watched Jessica stroll away. She also spotted her deputy head teacher, Miss Grey, walking over to the village green and head for the baking tent to help pin up the bunting. She certainly seemed keen!

Zaiba's glance shifted over to where a small group of children were chatting. She hoped they were talking about murder or espionage or something exciting like that! She hid a secret smile as she overheard a snatch of conversation:

"... but what will we be investigating? I hope it's a real crime!"

Peering over their shoulders at the sign-up sheet for her detective trail she could see five names written down. A good start! Zaiba had decided that entrants had to be less than twelve years of age, since she wanted to make the contest as fair as possible.

She plonked down her bag of detective trail equipment on the tarmac and pulled out her copy of *The Flower Show Felony* by her favourite writer of all time: Eden Lockett. Eden was a detective-turned-author and all her stories were based on true cases that she had investigated! Alongside her auntie, Eden Lockett was Zaiba's inspiration. *The Flower Show Felony* was set at a prestigious flower show. Zaiba had decided to base her detective trail on the story in the book. But instead of being set at a flower show, Zaiba had adapted the original story so it was based at the summer fete, and her

detectives didn't have to solve the crime of sabotage but
... murder!

Zaiba opened her huge bag and went through the
checklist of props one more time.

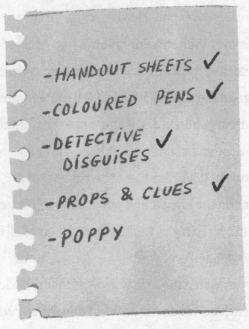

- HANDOUT SHEETS ✓
- COLOURED PENS ✓
- DETECTIVE DISGUISES ✓
- PROPS & CLUES ✓
- POPPY

She jerked her head up. "Hold on. Where's Poppy?"
She was one of Zaiba's most important props!

"Zai! Over here!"

As if on cue, Zaiba heard her best friend calling.
Turning round she saw Poppy in a bright blue dress

waving over to her from the entrance to the baking tent. Zaiba was always impressed by Poppy's outfit choices. Today she had paired her outfit with some lace-up ankle boots – practical and stylish.

Zaiba rushed over and gave her a hug. "Hey, Pops." She glanced around. "Where's your mum?"

"She's setting up for the dog show. You know how serious she gets about it! But listen, there are more important things to discuss." Poppy leaned in to whisper, "Guess who's in there, helping to set up the baking tent? Marco Romano!"

"Gabriele's dad?" Zaiba frowned. Why was that so important?

Poppy must have noticed the confusion on her face. "Yes, but – *much* more exciting! – he's married to the author of the book about unicorn cats – *Unicats*! I wonder if we could get a signed copy..."

"There's only one author I care about," Zaiba said, patting the yellow bag she always wore over her shoulder and felt her Eden Lockett book safely inside. She got out *The Flower Show Felony* and flicked to page thirty two.

"Another of your ammi's notes?" Poppy smiled.

All of the Eden Lockett books that Zaiba owned were first editions, inherited from her birth mum who she called Ammi. Zaiba had no memories of her birth mother, and had only recently found out that she'd been a top detective alongside Aunt Fouzia. The sisters had set up the Snow Leopard Detective Agency together! But on a secret mission when Zaiba was only a year old, her ammi had gone missing and passed away. Zaiba tried not to feel too sad about this and the notes her ammi made in the margins of the books certainly helped. They felt like the last tokens left to her from her mother and reading them was a way of getting to know her. Scribbles, notes and sometimes drawings that always seemed to come in useful at the right time.

Tracing her finger over the page, Zaiba read this particular note aloud: *"Think the unthinkable!"*

Poppy and Zaiba caught each other's eyes and laughed.

"That one has already come true!" Poppy said.

"Who would have thought we'd be in charge of the

first ever international branch of the Snow Leopard Detective Agency?" Zaiba said another silent *thank you* to Aunt Fouzia for trusting Poppy and Ali to help Zaiba run the UK branch. At the moment their headquarter was Zaiba's room, using her little desk to draw up their many plans, but they had big hopes for the future!

"And who would have thought you'd be setting up the treasure trail at our school fete?" Poppy added.

"Or –" a voice from behind them interrupted – "that your dad would win first prize in the baking competition?"

They turned round to see Hassan and Ali, aprons on and equipment at the ready. Hassan had changed into his chef's whites, ordered online for this very occasion, but Ali had categorically refused to wear his. Instead he was in his favourite oversized hoodie, despite the heat, with an apron tied over the top. He'd even clipped his long fringe back for health and safety reasons. They looked ready for business.

"We haven't won yet!" Ali nudged his dad, rolling his eyes.

"Oh, but we will." Hassan's eyes narrowed and Zaiba noticed, not for the first time, where her brother got his cheeky twinkle.

From inside the tent, a bossy voice floated out over the loudspeaker. "The baking competition will start in ten minutes. I repeat, ten minutes!"

Hassan and Ali shared a panicked look and in a flurry of white aprons they disappeared inside the tent. Zaiba had never seen her dad and brother move so fast. She and Poppy had to run to keep up with them.

It was baking time!

Poppy and Zaiba found some seats at the side of the tent while Hassan and Ali went 'backstage'. The preliminary rounds were a test to see who had the skills to go through to the final. It was a rapid-fire, fifteen-minute test of skill, precision and taste – and it all rested on a cake pop.

"What's a cake pop?" Poppy asked, eyeing up the little round balls on sticks up on the counter. "I can't believe there's a cake I've never heard of!"

"They're round pieces of cake sponge on lollipop

sticks!" Zaiba explained. "The judges provided these ones to make sure everyone starts with the same base. But Dad makes super yummy ones at home. I had them on my birthday cake last year – you ate them so fast you probably don't remember!" Zaiba's birthday cake last year was decorated entirely with cake pops!

The compere for the baking event was a tall man with such a loud, booming voice that he didn't need to use a microphone to get everyone in the tent to stop chatting.

"Welcome, guests. The first heat of the Cake Pop Preliminaries is about to begin! In this round, the bakers will be judged on their ability to decorate ten cake pops in fifteen minutes. The judges will be looking for uniformity, precision and taste. We have three heats and a total of nine teams! Only three will make it to this afternoon's final – the winner from each heat."

Zaiba's tummy lurched. Her dad and Ali *had* to make it through. They'd worked so hard for it!

"Please welcome our first three teams into the tent." The compere waved his hand towards the back of the tent where a big screen had been put up to make a backstage area. As the audience clapped politely, Hassan, Ali and a mother and daughter team took their place behind the counters. Zaiba thought she recognized the girl from the year below.

"I thought there were three teams?" Poppy wondered.

Miss Grey, who seemed to have appointed herself as backstage helper, zoomed behind the screen to see what the matter was. A few minutes later, and after much fussing from Miss Grey, the last team came out. It was a father and daughter team. They had been held up by some problems with the buttoning of their chef whites!

"Don't worry, Zai. Your dad will definitely get through." Poppy squeezed Zaiba's hand. "Look, they're starting!"

"Bakers, get set..." the compere looked at his watch, "and ... go!"

The three teams set about grouping together the ingredients they needed and gathering equipment. In all three teams the adults were taking the lead, telling the kids what to do next and which ingredients to use.

Hassan had instructed Ali to begin melting chocolate

in a saucepan with some butter, which he was doing with focused attention. He even had a thermometer dipped into the chocolate that he held aloft, checking the measurements at regular intervals.

They looked cool, calm and collected, especially compared to the chaos of the other teams. The competition had only been going five minutes and one of the girls was already covered in cocoa powder. Her mum on the other hand didn't seem to have touched *anything* but instead was deliberating over which whisk attachment to fix to the electric mixer. The father and daughter team had managed to drop all of their ingredients and were doubled over laughing as they tried to pick them up.

Zaiba cringed and when she looked over at Poppy, she noticed her best friend had her hands over her eyes.

"I can't watch!" Poppy winced.

Five minutes later, Hassan and Ali's cake pops were covered in a shiny chocolate ganache. The mother and daughter team had managed to coat each of their cake pops in a mixture of cocoa powder and pink icing, and from the looks of it were getting ready to attach tiny umbrellas to each one. And the third team ... Well, it was a cake-pop catastrophe. But at least they were having fun!

By the end of the fifteen minutes, there were thirty cake pops up on the countertops, twenty of which Zaiba would happily have devoured on the spot.

The Lady Mayor had come to judge the preliminary rounds. She wore a set of gleaming ceremonial chains around her neck, accessorized with a swipe of shockingly bright red lipstick.

"I think that's a new shade," Poppy whispered to Zaiba excitedly. "It's called *Red Velvet!*" She gave a dreamy sigh.

The Lady Mayor tried a cake pop from each of the competitor's plates. Each time she sniffed the cake, held it close to her eye and then popped it in her mouth – whole. After a moment of chewing she placed the lollipop stick down and moved on to the next, not giving away anything.

After she had swallowed and dabbed her mouth with a napkin, the compere approached with the microphone.

"Lady Mayor, have you made your final decision?" he asked seriously.

The Lady Mayor nodded and held the microphone to her mouth. "The winners of this heat, and going through to the final are ... Hassan and Ali! Well done."

The crowd burst into applause and Zaiba let out a huge sigh of relief. Hassan and Ali were through! Her dad was giving Ali a big high five but the baking tent team were ushering them along, keen to clear up ready for the next heat.

Zaiba and Poppy joined them by the entrance flaps of the tent.

"You're through to the final!" Zaiba smiled, giving her dad a hug.

"Well done, Ali." Poppy ruffled his long fringe, making Ali squirm.

"Through to the final." Hassan blew his cheeks out. "I wish Jessica could have seen us, but she was too busy at the face-painting stand to come and watch!"

The compere's booming voice interrupted their conversation. "Everyone, the second heat will be commencing in five minutes, that's five minutes!"

Hassan put his arms round the children. "Come on, let's go break the good news to your mum while the second heat is on. I can't wait to tell her!"

3
ALWAYS SECOND BEST

Jessica was thrilled to hear Hassan and Ali were in the final, but she didn't have long to chat as the line of children waiting to be painted as tigers, zebras and dogs was getting longer and longer. Hassan and Ali went back to the baking tent to watch the heats – they wanted to see who their competition would be – but Zaiba and Poppy stayed with Jessica for a while. They watched her transform the children with her artistic skills and helped out where they could.

When the queue had calmed down a bit, Poppy and Zaiba made their way back into the tent to catch the final heat of the baking competition. They joined Hassan and

Ali, who had a prime viewing spot.

Zaiba's aunt Raim and her (least favourite) cousin Mariam were busy working away. Aunt Raim had taken the *shouting orders and stressing* approach with Mariam and it seemed to be working, though it didn't look enjoyable. Mariam was weighing out tiny bowls full of cinnamon sugar and nutmeg while Raim frantically paced around whipping up butter and flinging spoons about the place.

Zaiba's dad waved at Raim but she kept her eyes on the countertop, whispering instructions under her breath to Mariam, who had a face like thunder.

"Mariam looks as cheerful as ever," Zaiba said. She didn't get on with her cousin, with whom she unfortunately shared a birthday! In fact at their last joint party Mariam had complained about the cake pop cake, saying it wasn't a 'real' birthday cake. And here she was decorating them! "Typical," Zaiba tutted.

When the fifteen minutes was up and the judging had taken place, Raim and Mariam were named the winners! It looked as though the final would be a brother–sister contest between Hassan and Raim.

Hassan's face dropped from a huge, toothy smile to a grimace. Zaiba followed his eyeline to where the shiny kitchen counters gleamed in the sunlight. The other team through to the grand final was hanging around at the central workstation.

"Marco Romano is in the final too..." he said under his breath, eyeing up the dark-haired man polishing a stainless-steel mixing bowl.

"Oh!" Poppy's eyes lit up. "Did you know his partner writes—"

Zaiba nudged her friend. "Not now, Pops."

Marco spotted them watching him and sauntered over, his unbuttoned salmon-pink shirt blowing open and one hand combing through his shiny black curls. He reached out the same hand for a handshake and Zaiba saw her dad hesitate.

"Hassan!" Marco announced, snatching Hassan's hand a *bit* too vigorously. "Good to see you're in the final three as well, mate. I'm glad to have at least one *worthy* opponent in the tent."

Over Marco's shoulder, Zaiba could see Aunt Raim and Mariam organizing their equipment. Fortunately they were so engrossed in sorting through their rolling pins and piping bags that they didn't hear Marco's insult. Zaiba was also secretly glad her cousin hadn't seen her yet either.

"Good to see you too. Nothing like a bit of healthy competition." Hassan smiled back, though Zaiba could see a muscle in his jaw twitching.

There was an awkward moment where the two men, still firmly gripping hands, stared at each other in silence.

"May the best team win!" Poppy chirped, which somehow made the situation a thousand times *more* awkward. Zaiba could have cut the atmosphere with a kitchen knife.

Luckily, Marco's son, Gabriele, called over from his counter. "Dad! Where did you put the marble rolling pin?" As she looked over, Zaiba was struck by how similar they looked. With his black ringlets and dark brown eyes, Gabriele was a mini replica of his dad.

Marco didn't turn round to acknowledge his son but the corner of his eye began to twitch. "How many times do I have to tell him?" he muttered. "We keep the rolling pin in the fridge to cool it." Then he swivelled on his heel and marched back to the workstation, not even sparing a glance at Raim, who had held out her hand to greet him.

Hassan shook his head as he watched Marco leave and shrugged at his sister. Aunt Raim merely rolled her eyes and then got back to business. It was as if they were used to this kind of behaviour from Marco Romano.

"Can you tell us what that was all about?" Zaiba whispered.

"Tell you? I'll show you." Hassan glanced quickly over to their workstation, where Ali was busy laying out the equipment and photographing every moment for posterity. Zaiba wondered how much room for photographs the newspaper had! "I have a little bit of time before the main competition starts. Come with me."

Zaiba really needed to set up for her detective trail but she'd never met anyone her dad didn't like before. Her detective instincts were buzzing. She had to find out what had gone on between her dad and Marco!

Hassan led Zaiba and Poppy back to the school building and into the main hall. This is where they had lunch on school days, but today trays of cloudy home-made lemonade were laid out on the canteen counter along with platters of sandwiches and cakes. The doors of the hall were propped open to let the breeze blow through.

"Cucumber sandwiches! My favourite!" Poppy dug a hand into her pocket and pulled out a sparkly purse. "Come on, everyone. I'll buy us some." She handed over her pocket money and they each nibbled a tiny triangle of sandwich.

The three of them hovered next to a little table where lemonade was being sold. Hassan treated them to a glass each and they glugged the lemonade down gratefully. The sun was high in the sky and it was getting very hot indeed. Zaiba knew that staying hydrated was important. She needed to stay alert and focused if she was going to be as good a detective as Aunt Fouzia.

"Why have you brought us here?" Zaiba put down her empty cup and looked around. It was only the school hall – Zaiba didn't think there would be anything interesting to find.

"Look up there." Hassan pointed to a wooden plaque high on the wall. He took another sip of his lemonade. "*That's* why Marco is so competitive."

Zaiba looked up at the plaque, feeling a little embarrassed. She'd walked past it so many times but had never actually stopped to read it. That went against one of Eden Lockett's golden rules for being a good secret agent. Rule number fifteen: *Take note of everything around you. The smallest detail could be the biggest clue!*

Now that she stopped to fully pay attention to the plaque, Zaiba noticed the same names cropped up again and again over the years, picked out in curly gold lettering – including her dad and her aunt. There was only one adult's name missing – Marco's. Zaiba knew from her dad's stories that he'd gone to school with Marco.

"Wow, you won a lot of prizes!" Poppy exclaimed, gazing up at the plaque.

"I did!" Hassan raised his eyebrows. "But that's not what I'm trying to show you. Look carefully. What's missing?"

"Marco!" Zaiba finally understood. "So that's why he's so competitive. He really wants to win for once!"

"Marco came second every year and he's a very sore loser," Hassan said, folding his arms. "He always has been."

"You went to school *here*?" Poppy's eyes grew so huge that Zaiba thought they'd pop out of her head. "But you're ... you're..." Poppy shook her head in wonderment and Zaiba gave an inward groan. She could guess what her best friend was going to say next. Poppy couldn't imagine that any grown-up had once been a child, going to the same school as them. "You're so ol—"

Zaiba slapped her hand over Poppy's mouth and smiled sweetly at her dad, who frowned in confusion. "Is everything all right, girls?"

"Yes, please carry on with what you were saying!" Slowly, carefully, Zaiba lowered her hand, giving Poppy a warning look.

"Every year Marco tried to win first place and every year he came second. Sometimes to me but sometimes to the other students, like your aunt Raim." Hassan sighed. "So now he's got a huge chip on his shoulder." He looked as though he felt sorry for Marco.

Zaiba grabbed her dad's hand and squeezed. "Thank you for explaining – but don't let him get to you. I know you and Ali are going to do *brilliantly* in the competition!"

Hassan looked down from the plaque and squeezed her hand back. "You're right! Anyway, it's all about having fun. Speaking of which, we should get back to the tent."

He crumpled up his paper cup and aimed for the recycling bin at the back of the hall. He tossed it through the air like a pro-basketball player but it just missed, hitting the rim and falling at the feet of a woman wearing a breezy yellow summer skirt.

"Oh no," Poppy whispered, backing behind Zaiba. "Your dad's going to be in trouble now!"

It was Celia Goremain, the new head teacher! She looked down at the paper cup at her feet, before making a big show of bending down to put it in the bin.

"Oops!" Hassan smiled at her. "Silly me."

Before Ms Goremain could say anything, another figure appeared in the doorway that led to the waiting area by the head teacher's office at the back of the school hall. It was the Lady Mayor. She must have been resting after all the cake chaos!

Ms Goremain led the Lady Mayor out of the small waiting area and into the hall. The two of them glided past Hassan to greet the crowd that had huddled by the lemonade. But Zaiba didn't miss the way the head teacher arched an eyebrow at Hassan as they passed, and when she looked up she saw her dad was blushing. Talk about a killer eyebrow! If eyebrows could give out lines to teach naughty students a lesson, Hassan would have been ordered to write *I must not litter the school hall* a hundred times over.

"Good morning, everyone!" Ms Goremain said into a microphone. "I hope you've been enjoying all the wonderful things we have on offer. We will be having a small ceremony to celebrate the thirtieth anniversary of the fete in five minutes, that's *five minutes*. Gather your refreshments and join us out by the main stage on the village green!"

Ms Goremain wasn't particularly tall but she was certainly commanding. As she made her way out of the school hall and over to the green, the crowd scurried to obediently follow her towards a small stage by the baking tent where an audience of adults and children was waiting. Ali was among them, along with Aunt Raim and Mariam. After all, their baking preparations were done. There were even some photo journalists, with big zoom lenses on their cameras.

"The press are here!" Poppy cried and immediately began smoothing down her dress. But the photographers weren't here to see Poppy. They began snapping away as they spotted the two women approaching the stage. The Lady Mayor's ornate gilt chain shone in the sunlight and the head teacher looked like a yellow daisy in her top and skirt as she smiled sweetly at the camera lenses.

"Wow, from the look on her face now, you'd have no idea she could be so fierce," Zaiba muttered as she watched Ms Goremain take to the stage. She had given her killer eyebrows some time off for the ceremony! Zaiba noticed that the photographers seemed to be focusing on the new head teacher, and the Lady Mayor looked a little put out. Zaiba supposed she was used to getting all the attention.

"Look! There's Mum and Bean! Back in a minute." Poppy darted over to them through the crowd. Bean was Poppy's family's miniature schnauzer and the happiest dog Zaiba had ever met. He wagged his tail eagerly as he saw Poppy coming over and Poppy's mum beamed down proudly at him.

Zaiba, Hassan and Ali went to join Jessica, who was close to the edge of the main stage. She was talking with one of the school governors who was wearing a shiny name badge that said 'Thomas Hanlon'. He had steel-silver hair, was immaculately groomed and was wearing a smart pinstriped suit in navy blue. Beside him was the deputy head teacher, Miss Grey, who could almost have dressed to match him in her striped jumpsuit. Zaiba saw Miss Grey every day at school – she taught her science – but she had no idea what a school governor did. Thomas

Hanlon always seemed to be around when there were special events at the school or award ceremonies so Zaiba assumed he was some sort of school VIP.

"There's certainly more press here than usual," Jessica said to Mr Hanlon and Miss Grey. "They must want to hear more from Celia. I heard she's an exceptional head teacher – no wonder she got fast-tracked into the position here!"

"Oh yes, she's *very* talented," Miss Grey replied in an almost sarcastic tone.

Thomas Hanlon grunted.

What's their problem? Zaiba wondered, her skin prickling with suspicion. She couldn't understand how anyone could be grumpy on a day like today.

They all watched as the Lady Mayor took to the main stage and lifted a huge pair of scissors from a nearby table. She held them aloft, smiling. Zaiba had a full view of her gown. It was forest-green with red silk roses sewn all over it, and she'd completed the outfit with a matching rose pinned into her white hair.

At the back of the stage, a small jazz trio were

positioned, ready to strike up. Their eyes were pinned on the Lady Mayor as she raised the giant scissors. "It is my honour to be part of the thirty-year celebrations for this fete!" She gazed around the crowd, watching her. "You are all a key part of this and I am excited to see what the day holds!" Everyone cheered. "All money raised is going to the School Trust, please give generously!"

There was a worrying few seconds where the Lady Mayor struggled with the scissors before – *snip!* – she finally sliced through the ceremonial ribbon and it fluttered to the floor of the stage. The band leader nudged his colleagues and they burst into a rendition of some sort of jive, the music playing through speakers positioned around the village green and school grounds.

"Come on!" Ali said to their dad. "Before we know it, the competition will be starting. This is serious!" The two of them ran off back to the baking tent, not even bothering to say goodbye.

As the audience drifted away, heading towards the stalls and tents, Zaiba spotted her best friend in the crowd and called over to her. "Poppy, come on! It's time to get our detective trail under way!" She turned to her stepmum. "Are you ready?"

"Ready as I'll ever be!" Jessica said as Poppy ran to join them. The three of them had been planning this next stage ever since Aunt Fouzia had brilliantly suggested it, and had done two practice runs at home.

It was time to make murder look deadly.

4
MURDER SHE PAINTED

Jessica leaned back, wiping her hands on a damp flannel. Zaiba stood beside her, inspecting the handiwork.

"So?" Poppy asked. "How do I look?"

"No talking!" Jessica had warned. "Not until the blood dries."

Poppy heaved a sigh and picked up the hand mirror that was lying on the table beside Jessica's face paints. She let out a strangulated sound as she caught sight of herself in the glass. If her face hadn't already been painted a deadly white, Zaiba would have sworn the blood was draining from her friend's cheeks.

"It's brilliant," Zaiba said, kissing her stepmum on the

cheek. "She looks exactly like a murder victim. Thank you!"

Jessica was already rearranging her face paints to bring out some of the less ... bloody colours. Sparkling pink, neon-green and tiger-orange. Another queue was already forming at the stand and one of the little boys was staring hard at Poppy.

"You're not going to make me like that, are you?" he whimpered. "I wanted to be a lion."

Jessica laughed. "Don't worry," she said as Poppy returned the mirror. "There's only one person here who's allowed to look like death warmed up."

"Are you ready?" Zaiba asked, linking arms with her best friend. "Our detectives are waiting." The two of them wandered across the playground. "Detectives disperse!" According to her cue, Poppy began to wander away from Zaiba as though she'd suddenly become hugely interested in a cherry tree beside the railings. But little did anyone else know – Poppy was moving to her designated position, just like they'd agreed. It was time to begin!

Zaiba pasted on her most serious face and glanced round the group of soon-to-be detectives gathered by the fete table. Beyond their shoulders, she could see the Soak the Teacher stand and another stall where people were trying to guess how many sweets were in a giant glass jar. She quickly counted heads and was thrilled to realize that hers was the most popular stand!

"What you're about to witness," she said, in her best serious tone, "may be difficult for those of you with a weak stomach."

Ten worried faces peered back at her. The children were dressed in an array of disguises: A bowler hat, some oversized glasses, a multi-coloured bow tie, a fake nose/moustache combo and several of them were wearing wigs. It was fun to see how the accessories she'd picked out made her fellow pupils look totally different! One of the detectives was wearing a white cape back to front, which made her look like a ghost. Wow! They were really going for it!

"Are you ready to witness ..." her voice lowered to a whisper, "a *murder*?"

A few brave heads nodded.

"Come on then!" Zaiba clutched her hands behind her back and led them round a corner of the school playground to where Poppy lay ... dead on the tarmac.

Well, pretend dead of course.

The previous day the two of them had come there before the light faded. Zaiba had ordered Poppy to lie down and "Just play dead!" It had been a bit tricky at first as Poppy had insisted on crossing her arms over her chest, which Zaiba thought was very unlikely for a murder victim. Eventually she'd managed to persuade her friend to let her limbs flail out across the tarmac. Then she'd outlined Poppy's body position in chalk.

As she gazed down at her now, Zaiba was glad Jessica had used a whole tube of fake red blood. Poppy looked really convincing!

Zaiba turned to her detectives. One of the younger contestants, a small boy from Class 1A, was starting to look a bit green.

"Can anyone work out the cause of death?" Zaiba asked gravely.

"OOHHHHH, the pain!" Poppy suddenly started wailing, making Zaiba jump. "This can't be the end, I'm too young!"

Zaiba gave a loud, pointed cough. Now wasn't the time for dramatics – murder victims couldn't talk!

A boy in a wig cleared his throat, staring at Poppy's prone figure on the ground. "It looks to me like poison."

Zaiba shook her head. "That seems unlikely... Look at the body, what might the blood and open wounds suggest?" Jessica had drawn a particularly gory wound on Poppy's upper arm. "Anyone else?"

"Strangulation?" the girl in the bowler hat asked hopefully.

Zaiba struggled to hold in a sigh of disappointment. Clearly not everyone was born with a detective's eye. "Do you see any bruises?" She pointed at Poppy's throat, where there weren't any marks. The rest of the group leaned in to have a closer look.

Zaiba glanced at the curious faces. "Any other ideas?"

A girl's hand shot into the air. "Stabbing?"

At last! "Correct. That's the first stage of the victim profile complete." Zaiba handed out pens and paper. "It's now up to all of you to find the evidence hidden around the fete. You'll need to have your eyes peeled for anything that strikes you as unusual, unexpected or just plain suspicious."

"Can you give us some examples?" said one boy, a pen gripped above his notebook. He pushed his fake glasses back up the bridge of his nose.

"Good question." Zaiba sucked on her lip, thinking. She wanted to help them, without giving away the clues entirely. After all, she could never have become a real detective if Aunt Fouzia hadn't initially helped her. "Here are three things to look out for. Objects that look out of place, people behaving suspiciously and signs of ... murder!" She grinned as she watched the detectives' eyes grow wide. "The clues you find will help you piece together the crime to reveal what happened and who did it. The riddles on your activity sheet will lead you to each clue. OK, good luck, detectives. Your time starts ..." she looked at the time on her watch, "NOW!"

In ones and twos, the children dashed off in different directions, clutching their activity sheets and, in some cases, their stomachs.

After a moment Poppy slowly opened an eye. "Can I be alive now? I'm worried the blood will get on my new dress."

Zaiba helped her up and the two girls high-fived, confident that they would do Aunt Fouzia proud. Zaiba and Poppy had put a lot of work into setting up the trail. They just had to do a final check of their clues.

They'd already put each clue in a particular place around the park and school grounds, to act as evidence for the contestants to find. Among the most crucial pieces of evidence were a red bloodstain on one of the stepping stones in the pond, a felt dagger in the science room bin, and confession letters, which they'd hidden in the bird boxes.

They'd had so much fun writing the letters! Poppy had added a little splatter of blood (red ink) beside each signature. Zaiba had made sure each letter began with the perfect introduction – *For You, Mr Policeman* or *This is the perfect criminal speaking*... They'd even composed one letter from words cut out of a newspaper! All the competitors had to do was work out the riddles, find the clues and solve the murder. Then they could officially call themselves detectives! Well, almost. Zaiba could have completed this trail of clues in a few minutes, but she knew not everyone had her laser-sharp mind.

"Oh, one more thing!" Poppy announced, producing a small bottle of red glitter and sprinkling it on the stone.

Zaiba raised her eyebrows.

"What? We don't want people to think it's actual blood! It's only a pretend clue." Poppy had a point – Zaiba didn't want anyone to actually get arrested for Poppy's fake murder at the school fete. This was meant to be fun!

"Let's check that the other clues are still in place," Zaiba said. "Before our budding detectives get to them."

The pair worked quickly. There was the scrap of fabric on a gatepost – in place! The cracked flowerpot containing an earring – perfect! And the footprint by the corner of the biggest oak tree on the village green. Poppy had been most excited about the footprint. She had used one of her mum's designer shoes to make it, pressing the heel into the grass. Now Zaiba bent down and pushed the little sign she had placed next to the footprint more firmly into the earth. She had decided it was a good idea to place a tiny sign next to each clue that read 'DO NOT MOVE'. The signs weren't big enough to give away the hiding places, but just big enough to stop the clues being moved if someone stumbled across them. Zaiba couldn't risk the trail being disrupted. Not only would it ruin her chances of this going down in history as the **Best Fete Treasure Trail Ever** but Aunt Fouzia might reconsider letting her head up the Snow Leopard Detective Agency UK!

"Let's check on our last clue." Zaiba pulled a small bottle out of her props bag. It contained more blood-red ink. She nodded towards the gardener's shed – somewhere hardly anyone visited.

"Perfect!" Poppy cried. The spurts of blood from a ferocious stabbing were running down her face in the heat. She looked a little bit like a vampire after a particularly juicy feast.

They raced over to the shed by the rose gardens and found the grassy patch where they'd hidden a bloodstained handkerchief. Zaiba peered at it. The fake blood had dried and didn't look as gory as it had when they'd first covered it in ink.

"Just a little more..." She added some fresh splatters of blood, then wiped her hands on her denim shorts. "This is going to be great!"

She stuck her DO NOT MOVE sign beside the mound of grass. As she straightened up she heard a jangling of keys. "Quick! Hide!" she shouted in a whisper.

She and Poppy leaped round the side of the shed. Had one of their teams finished the trail this quickly? Had she made it *too* easy? She didn't want anyone spotting them – the competitors might realize there were important clues nearby!

The jangling sound grew louder and Zaiba peeked out. It wasn't the young detectives. It was the school caretaker, Peter, jogging straight past them. He was chasing after three figures as they strolled towards the baking tent! His large set of keys was hanging off his belt, still rattling as he slowed to walk beside the people he was following, the baking competition judges – Celia Goremain, Thomas Hanlon and the Lady Mayor.

Zaiba knew Peter on sight. She'd once found herself locked in the school P.E. cupboard after investigating a suspicious spate of missing rounders balls. After banging on the locked cupboard door for what felt like forever, Peter had come to release her, looking surprised to find her trapped there. Fortunately, Zaiba had been able to quickly come up with an excuse about volunteering to help tidy up the beanbags.

"Do you think he saw us?" Poppy whispered.

Peter seemed to be talking intensely to the judges and Zaiba straightened up, stepping out from behind the shed. "I don't think he has eyes for anyone other than those three," she said. "I wonder what's so important."

They could still hear the keys jangling from his belt.

"How does he remember what each key is for?"

Zaiba wondered aloud.

Poppy shrugged. "I don't know, but those definitely wouldn't be my choice of belt accessories!"

They heard Peter's voice as he approached the group. "Hello all!" he panted.

The head teacher raised one of her killer eyebrows. "What is it, Peter? We have somewhere to be."

He gave them a wide, hopeful grin then suddenly dropped back so he was walking beside the Lady Mayor. "Don't suppose you fancy coming on a tour of the rose garden? I've been working quite hard on it this season and I think the school should be very proud of our progress."

As he spoke, Zaiba noticed that he only seemed to be looking at the Lady Mayor. Not looking – staring. His smile widened, as though he could convince her with the strength of his sparkling white teeth.

"Not the rose garden *again*," Ms Goremain muttered, a little too loudly. Peter's face dropped. She must have noticed his devastated look as she quickly added, "I mean that the, uh, baking competition is about to begin and we really mustn't be late." The three judges quickened their pace, but so did Peter.

He turned his attention back to the Lady Mayor, his gaze travelling down the hand-stitched flowers. "That's a really lovely dress, Lady Mayor. It would look even lovelier next to my roses in the garden. Are you sure you don't have a moment to come and take a look?"

The Lady Mayor laughed shakily and Zaiba noticed her fiddling with her chain of office. "Thank you, but we really must get ready to begin the judging. We wouldn't want to keep the contestants waiting!" Before Peter could respond, she turned and strode off with Ms Goremain and Thomas Hanlon.

Peter slowed to a halt beside a storage unit on the edge of the green and watched the judges draw ahead. A dark look came over the caretaker's face before he took a deep breath, kicking a foot against the grass so hard that he loosened some turf and created a gap beneath the door to the storage unit. He shook his head and muttered something, then stormed off towards the school hall.

"Now *that* was weird." Poppy sighed. "Why was Ms

Goremain so against going to see the roses? Peter was only trying to be nice. I wish someone would offer to show me around the rose garden!"

Zaiba looked at her, confused. "But you know you get hay fever."

Poppy drew herself up to her fullest height. "That wouldn't matter, I'd carry a box of tissues with me!"

Zaiba thought back over what they'd witnessed. How annoyed the head teacher had seemed, how the Lady Mayor's face had flushed with embarrassment ... and how angry Peter had looked to be spurned. Zaiba was sure something suspicious was going on. Why was Peter trying to distract them right as the baking competition was about to start? Why did the head teacher say such an unkind thing about his rose garden? And why had the Lady Mayor seemed so embarrassed by his attention? He was just proud of his accomplishments.

"What do you think it all means, Poppy?" Zaiba turned to her friend. "Do you think there's a mystery here?"

Poppy shook her head firmly, sending out a fine spray of melted fake blood. "Definitely not. No mystery at all. It just shows adults are strange and we know that already."

Poppy was right, of course. Zaiba should never have allowed herself to get distracted. There was a much more important detective trail to think about, the one that would be the best activity at the whole school fete... The one Zaiba had created!

5
CAN'T STAND THE HEAT?

> • all clues in place ✓
> • Poppy's pretend murder ✓
> • detective trail contestants set off for first clues ✓
> • Poppy washed off her melted face-paint bloodbath ✓

Everything was going to plan.

So why did Zaiba feel an uncertain fluttering in her stomach?

She found herself looking over at the baking tent and realized she wanted to check on her dad and Ali — she knew they'd be nervous. Hassan had barely got any sleep last night, although he'd never admit it was because of pre-competition jitters.

"Come on, Pops. We have time to kill. Ha, kill! Get it? Let's check on Dad and Ali."

Poppy rolled her eyes. "Please don't try to make jokes, Zaiba. That's Ali's job." She grinned. "Hey! Maybe there'll be some baking to sample." Poppy rubbed her hands together. It must have been at least half an hour since she'd last had a snack.

Together they headed across the green towards the baking tent, hopping over the guy ropes that had been hammered into the grass with wooden stakes. The tent had two peaked points on the canvas roof that made it look like a circus tent and the entrance flaps had been tied open. But before Zaiba and Poppy could enter, somebody crashed into them — somebody wearing a very strong aftershave!

"Oh, pardon me—" The figure paused as he caught sight of Zaiba. It was Marco, racing out of the tent with a wild look in his eyes, apron flying in the wind.

He threw his hands into the air in frustration. "The equipment here is so second-rate. It just won't do for my special glaze!" Without waiting for a response, he ran off across the green, heading in the direction of the school.

Zaiba frowned. "Surely, that's not in the rules!" She felt angry on her dad's behalf. People couldn't leave the baking tent to go and get extra equipment! She had made her detective trail as fair as possible – the other competitions at the fete should do the same.

Zaiba and Poppy peered through the entrance of the tent to see a small crowd sitting on chairs, eagerly waiting for the final to begin. No one else seemed bothered about Marco's dramatic exit.

Zaiba observed the workstations. Ali and Hassan were working at a tall counter to the far left of the tent, Aunt Raim and Mariam were in the middle and Gabriele (minus his dad for the time being) was on the right. Each counter had a food mixer with various shiny attachments. In a tray beside it was every type of utensil under the sun.

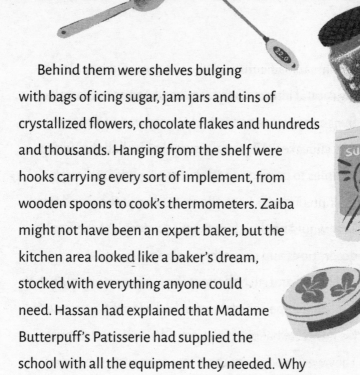

Behind them were shelves bulging with bags of icing sugar, jam jars and tins of crystallized flowers, chocolate flakes and hundreds and thousands. Hanging from the shelf were hooks carrying every sort of implement, from wooden spoons to cook's thermometers. Zaiba might not have been an expert baker, but the kitchen area looked like a baker's dream, stocked with everything anyone could need. Hassan had explained that Madame Butterpuff's Patisserie had supplied the school with all the equipment they needed. Why had Marco needed to go rushing off for something else?

"How does this baking competition work, anyway?" Poppy whispered. "I can't see any ovens."

Zaiba thought back to how she, Ali, Jessica and her dad had huddled on the sofa the previous week, going through the rules one last time. A baker could never be too prepared, Hassan had informed them. Just like a detective. Then he'd flipped open his school baking competition planner and turned to the front page.

Hassan had written down the competition rules in big capital letters. Each team had been asked to bake their cupcakes at home, and Hassan had baked over fifty cupcakes! All to make sure that he had the perfect samples to bring on the day. If they made it through their preliminary heat, they would be in the grand final. That would be their last chance to complete the final decorations and prove their baking prowess.

Hassan and Ali had spent three weeks perfecting their cupcake recipe, which Hassan had adapted from one of his favourite bakers of all time – Madame Butterpuff. They were working with a Genoise sponge, which he was giving a Pakistani twist by infusing the mixture with cardamom. He was convinced he'd nailed the balance of sweet to aromatic – at least that's what he'd told Zaiba and Jessica about one thousand times.

Hassan had read aloud the requirements in a big, booming voice, rather like the announcer at the hockey games he loved watching on TV.

"The cupcakes shall be judged on:

Taste

Texture

Presentation

Uniformity

Creativity

Plus, a SURPRISE TECHNICAL CHALLENGE!"

The rules were super strict!

"What if we can't do all that?" Ali had asked in a quiet voice, and Hassan had drawn him into a hug, kissing the top of his son's head before he'd had the chance to wriggle away.

"We'll do our best," Hassan had said. No one can ask for more than that."

In the baking tent, Zaiba and Poppy found some empty chairs at the back and sat down. This was the perfect place to watch discreetly.

"The technical challenge, for bonus points," said the compere, wearing a black suit and a dicky bow, "is to see if each team can produce perfect fondant icing bows to sit alongside your cakes. We want the icing bow to be *exactly* 1.5 cm wide." His eyes narrowed. "But rulers aren't allowed." The audience gasped, but he moved on.

"Of course, you'll also need to decorate the cupcakes to the highest standard." Zaiba felt a shiver pass over her body. In all their practice runs, Hassan and Ali had used fondant to make flowers, balloons, cherry stalks ... but never a bow! And to expect them to judge 1.5 cm without a ruler – that was just cruel!

"Make that bow 1 cm wide and you won't get a handshake from the judges." Hassan winked at Ali, making the audience giggle. Ali flicked a silver sugar ball back at his dad and the compere looked disapprovingly at them.

While the compere was distracted, Raim was staring daggers over at Gabriele's counter. Mariam was staring hard at the countertop, her cheeks flaming.

"Goodness!" Poppy whispered. "Mariam's mum is super competitive."

And she wasn't the only one who had noticed. Perched in front of Zaiba and Poppy were the parents of one of Zaiba's classmates. She recognized them from school pick-up time. They were speaking to each other in hushed voices but because Zaiba and Poppy were so close they could make out what the parents were saying.

"To goad a child ... that's not good," the dad tutted.

"Exactly. I know Marco and Raim are both competitive, but really – the kids seem embarrassed by them!" the mum whispered back.

Poppy and Zaiba exchanged a look. Zaiba and her cousin didn't get along, and Mariam always tried to get Zaiba into trouble – she had been especially difficult when Zaiba was investigating the case of the missing diamond collar. Even so, Zaiba had felt sorry for her cousin by the end – Mariam was lonely and wanted to make friends. She just didn't show it very often. It didn't help that Raim was a super-strict mum and she was being totally embarrassing and competitive in front of everyone!

"I'm surprised Raim even showed her face here today," the mum continued. "After that huge row she had yesterday morning with the new head." She shook her head. "All because Mariam got moved down a set in maths."

Zaiba's heart sank.

"Did you hear that the argument only ended after she challenged Ms Goremain to recite the first fifty digits in Pi," the dad whispered.

Both parents' shoulders shook with silent laughter. Zaiba had no idea that adults could be so gossipy. Now she understood why Aunt Fouzia always made new clients sign a confidentiality form – three times over! What was it she always said to Zaiba? *Loose lips sink ships.* Even the biggest ship wasn't safe from these parents!

Zaiba peered over their heads and saw that the cake decorating had started. Mariam and her mum were painstakingly placing individual sprinkles on to their cupcakes with a pair of tweezers. Raim only ever accepted perfection. *Poor Mariam!* Zaiba could see her cousin's hands trembling and a sprinkle go skittering across the counter. Once again, she felt a wave of sympathy for Mariam – she looked miserable. Zaiba caught her eye and gave her a little wave but Mariam scowled and looked away. *Fine*, Zaiba thought, *I was only trying to be nice.*

"I would be too nervous to hold those tweezers

steady." Poppy puffed out her cheeks. "Especially with the judges breathing down my neck!"

Even as Poppy said this, two of the judges moved from one counter to the next, staring hard at the competitors stirring frantically. The head teacher raised one of her killer eyebrows when she saw that Gabriele was using a metal spoon and scribbled a note on her clipboard. Thomas Hanlon was shaking his head.

"I know," Zaiba said, her gaze still trained on the judging. "Pathologists have loads of training to use tweezers—"

"So do beauticians!" Poppy added.

"Exactly! That's my point," she said, indicating the stage. "Mariam can't be expected to be perfect."

The only person who looked more miserable than Mariam was Gabriele, who was standing alone at his counter, looking lost without his dad.

The Lady Mayor suddenly appeared alongside the other judges. She was holding a rose-coloured silk fan and wafting her face as she took long strides up and down the workstations, inspecting each team's progress.

Poppy gave a running commentary, doing her best impression of the compere: "And following the Lady Mayor is our second judge, head teacher Ms Goremain in a stunning yellow skirt and, oooh are those vintage Mariella sandals? Anyway, following closely behind is the third judge ... uh, some guy I don't know but who we saw acting strangely earlier!"

"That's Thomas Hanlon," Zaiba said. "He's the school governor."

"What's that?"

"I'm not entirely sure." Zaiba got out her Eden Lockett notebook and jotted down *School governor* followed by a question mark. A good detective made sure to fill in any gaps in their knowledge.

The three judges arrived at Gabriele's counter and his look of worry intensified.

"Young man," the Lady Mayor bellowed, looking out over the audience. "Where is your team mate?"

Zaiba could have told her where he was – somewhere in the school! She wondered for a moment if she should say something but then thought better of it. *I'm related to more than one of the contestants. I don't want the judges to accuse me of interfering.*

Gabriele opened his mouth and then closed it again like a fish, completely at a loss for words. But before he could try to speak again, there was a scuffle behind Zaiba and Marco burst through the entrance of the tent, sweating profusely.

"I'm here!" he sang in a carefree voice. Everyone in the audience turned to look as Marco rushed up to his counter, clutching a small bowl in his hands.

"And what *exactly* have you been doing out there?" the Lady Mayor asked, her eyes narrowing.

A bead of sweat tracked down Marco's face. "I was ... I was..." A beam of sunlight shone through the entrance. "I was warming my butter in the sun!" Marco ran his hand through his hair again, though Zaiba noticed it tremble slightly.

The Lady Mayor's face flushed. "Warming your butter ... in the sun?!" She gazed out across the crowd and there was a snort of laughter from the parents.

Marco wiped the sweat from his face with a corner of

a tea towel. "Yes! Didn't you know that sun-melted butter tastes twenty-four per cent better in a buttercream frosting?"

Zaiba noticed Ali freeze at his counter. Her brother was a walking encyclopaedia of facts and he *knew* when a statistic was false, or made up! Raim was watching Marco closely too.

But by this time, Marco was shooting a toothy smile at the judges and was carrying on as if nothing had happened. He was so confident, they weren't sure what to do and let him get on with it!

"But he told us he was looking for better equipment," Zaiba muttered.

Poppy nodded her head hard in agreement. "He's fibbing! Surely that's against the rules?"

Zaiba blinked hard. It most definitely was! Something here wasn't right... She couldn't work out what though and was soon distracted by the competition.

Marco had leaped straight back into action and was frantically whipping his frosting. He was stirring so hard that each time the spoon hit the side of the metal bowl it made a loud *ding!* Gabriele was trying not to flinch and drop the delicate flower petals he was arranging on a cupcake. Zaiba was practically holding her breath watching his hands shake.

"We come now to team Raim. Hey, that rhymes!" The compere made himself chuckle. He stood next to Raim, who was ignoring him and busily getting on with her piping.

"Have you attempted this particular recipe at home before?" the compere asked, holding the mic right under Raim's nose.

"Of course I have! I would never come to a competition unprepared." Raim grumbled. "Now would you leave me in peace?"

Poppy nudged Zaiba and pointed at Mariam, who had turned bright red.

"Right," the compere murmured. "Let's check in with team Hassan."

"And Ali!" Ali protested, speaking into the mic.

"What do you think your chances are this year?" the compere asked Ali.

Ali thought for a moment, holding his spatula aloft. "Thirty-three point three per cent recurring, or a one in three chance."

The compere blinked. "OK…"

All three teams had progressed and were piping their designs on to the cupcakes. As part of the judging was based on presentation, Zaiba guessed that intricate piping work would be key to judging the winner. She hoped that her dad and Ali were also managing to cut their fondant icing strips to exactly 1.5 cm for those extra points! She was too far away from the workstations to see exactly how Hassan and Ali's cakes were doing, but something else caught her eye. Poppy must have been reading Zaiba's mind (they were best friends after all) because she noticed it too.

"What's Miss Grey doing hovering by the fridge?" she whispered. "She looks so awkward!"

"Or she's a control freak and she wants to keep an eye on everyone…" Zaiba whispered back.

But before Zaiba could ponder any further there was a beep from her Eden Lockett watch – it was time to check on the detective trail contestants.

"Are we on schedule?" Poppy whispered. They'd run through the trail's itinerary countless times.

Zaiba shrugged. "We'll know when we find our detectives. With any luck, the teams should now be heading to clue two."

A loud horn sounded in the tent, making Zaiba jump.

"Time's up!" the compere announced. "Down tools! Competitors, bring your cupcakes to the stage and arrange them on the presentation plates. Judges, take your place – you will be blindfolded in preparation for the blind tasting."

"I wish we could stay a bit longer!" Poppy exclaimed. "I was looking forward to watching the blind tasting and seeing who wins. We might even get to try some of the cakes!"

Zaiba sighed. "I know. But it's our duty to make sure the detective trail runs smoothly. Aunt Fouzia made me promise, and besides – I can't wait to see how the first event organized by the UK branch of the Snow Leopard Detective Agency is going!"

Poppy gave a big smile. "Me too!"

"It's got to run smoothly – we have our reputation to protect." She took her friend's hand. "Come on! We can taste the icing later."

As the bakers stepped away from their workstations and moved towards the stage, Zaiba and Poppy crept out of the tent and squinted in the bright sunlight, before setting off to where they expected the contestants should be at this stage. Zaiba hoped that by training up some of her classmates in detective skills she might generate some potential recruits for the Snow Leopard Detective Agency UK. You could never be too vigilant and having more than three detectives in the village would surely lower the frequency of crimes. Not that there were many crimes in Beckley.

They were heading towards the green, where they'd left the second clue, when a blood-curdling sound sent shivers down Zaiba's spine. Poppy stumbled to a halt, gripping her friend's hand even tighter.

"What was that?" Zaiba could hear the tremble in Poppy's voice.

The sound wasn't a horn this time or the jazz trio playing on the main stage. It was the type of noise she'd only ever heard before in detective programmes or imagined as she read an Eden Lockett novel with a torch beneath her duvet. Except this time the sound was more real, more panicked ... more terrifying.

It was the sound of someone screaming!

And it was coming from the baking tent.

6
DETECTIVES COMING THROUGH!

Zaiba and Poppy stared at each other, frozen to the spot.

"A real-life murder!" Poppy cried. "It has to be!"

But who would commit murder over a baking competition? The prize wasn't *that* big.

"Let's not get ahead of ourselves," Zaiba said. The first rule of detecting was to stay calm at all times. Even so, the two of them broke into a sprint back to the baking tent.

"Clear the way," Poppy called ahead. "Detectives coming through!"

Zaiba scoured the tent, looking for her dad and Ali.

Were they OK?

"Oh, thank goodness." There they were – standing at  their workstation, hands by their sides, mouths hanging open. They were staring at something and as Zaiba followed their eyeline she saw someone on the stage clutching their throat, a cupcake in their hand with one huge bite taken out of it.

It was Ms Goremain!

The new head teacher was gasping for air, her eyes bulging as she coughed and spluttered. She had pulled off her blindfold, and in one hand she was gripping the half-eaten cupcake so hard that pink icing oozed out between her fingers. The rose-petal decoration fell to the ground along with the fondant bow. The scream must have come from her!

"She's choking!" someone cried.

A group of people rushed round her, including Zaiba and Poppy.

"I'm not choking," she spluttered between ragged

breaths. With her spare hand, she waved the bystanders away. "I am having a severe reaction to ... *something*! Please, I need some air. I think I need medical help!" Even as she spoke, Zaiba could see a bright flush spreading down the head teacher's throat and her eyes were turning red as she wheezed and spluttered.

In an instant, Miss Grey pushed through the throng of onlookers. The deputy head stood before Ms Goremain and tied her hair back into a hasty bun, before rolling up the sleeves of her dress.

"I'm not sure it's the best time to adjust her outfit," Poppy whispered to Zaiba. But Zaiba knew what Miss Grey was doing – she was getting ready to give the head teacher proper medical attention. She'd seen this before on the weekly medical drama Jessica loved to watch.

"Give her air! Give her air, please!" Miss Grey shooed the crowd away before leading Ms Goremain off the stage and over to a fold-out chair, gently lowering her down so she could sit.

"Put your head between your knees – now!" Ms Goremain did as she was told and slumped forwards, still gripping the cupcake in one hand. The deputy head prised the rose-petal cake from between the head teacher's fingers and placed it back on a plate, before turning to the bystanders. "All right, everyone, stand back! I'll take it from here," she barked. "The competition is off! Bakers – report to the school hall and wait there. Everyone else, please vacate the tent. Immediately!"

Zaiba turned to watch the crowd disperse. Among the group was a man with a white apron and a red face – Marco. His eyes bulged as though *he* was the one who had suffered a reaction. "Outrageous!" He flung a tea towel on to the ground and stormed out of the tent, Gabriele trailing after him.

Mariam and her mum were next to leave. Raim was furiously whispering instructions into Mariam's ear and as they passed, Zaiba heard her hiss, "Did you put the butter back in the fridge? Tell me you did!"

Mariam definitely whimpered as she shook her head.

"Goodness," Zaiba said. "It's only a baking competition."

Mariam's mum must have heard her because she turned slowly on the spot and glared at Zaiba. "It's never *only* a competition, Zaiba!"

"Sorry, Auntie," Zaiba muttered, staring hard at a dandelion in the grass. When she dared to look up again, she saw Hassan and Ali slowly removing their white aprons and leaving them on the counter. It nearly broke Zaiba's heart to see them forced to abandon their hard work but she knew that bigger issues were at hand, whatever Aunt Raim said. She glanced at Ms Goremain again. Her face was getting redder and Zaiba's detective instincts whirred into action. An allergic reaction? Or toxic poisoning? She had recently read about a case like this in Eden Lockett's *Death By Doughnuts*.

The rest of the crowd filed out of the tent but Zaiba pulled Poppy over to stand beside one of the canvas walls. "Let's wait here. See what we can spot." It was all well and good setting up a pretend detective trail, but Zaiba had been aching to solve a real-life mystery ever since she'd reunited celebrity Maysoon with her Italian greyhound and its diamond collar. This could be the mystery she'd been waiting for!

As the crowd pushed past, the girls overhead someone mutter, "Miss Grey's finally got a chance to play at being the boss. She's been waiting for this moment a long time..." Parents certainly liked gossiping! But Zaiba had to admit that the deputy head had taken charge and started throwing around orders almost immediately.

Poppy and Zaiba turned to each other and nodded in unison. "Control freak."

A kerfuffle broke out by the entrance as the stream of people exiting the tent stumbled into the group of journalists and photographers from earlier who were trying to force their way in, despite the fact that everyone had been ordered to leave. Some of them held their cameras above their heads, trying to snap photos of the red-in-the-face Ms Goremain. How rude! Others were hurling questions at anyone who would listen.

"They really should leave if that's what people have been told to do," Poppy commented, folding her arms.

But Zaiba couldn't help a pulse of sympathy with the journalists. They were only trying to get to the bottom of this mystery and she knew how that felt.

"Did you see anything suspicious?" A journalist shoved his microphone into a parent's face.

The dad spluttered. "Well, it looked like the competitors were using stainless steel bowls?"

The reporter whipped round, wasting no more time on such a silly answer. Zaiba couldn't blame him! "Is it true that the new head teacher has food allergies?" he questioned someone else.

The mother shrugged. "All I know from my daughter is that Ms Goremain changed Wednesday snack treats from cookies to fresh fruit."

But this clearly wasn't the answer the journalist was looking for either. Details of the school's snack menu wasn't going to help get to the bottom of the strange turn of events in the baking tent.

"That journalist needs Aunt Fouzia to help him," Zaiba muttered. "She'd know the right questions to ask."

Up on the main stage outside the baking tent, Zaiba could just about make out the Lady Mayor. She was standing on tiptoe, looking like she was about to say something as she watched the parents being questioned. Zaiba expected her to call off the journalists but instead she threw her hands into the air and began wailing. It was almost as though she was trying to draw attention to herself.

"Oh, dear me! What a disaster!" she cried in a loud voice. She dragged a hand over her brow. "And to think it could have been *me* suffering from such a terrible reaction!" She peeped out from beneath her hand to see if the journalists were listening. "What on earth would the village do without its Lady Mayor?"

"Get a new one?" Poppy said under her breath, but Zaiba shushed her.

If the Lady Mayor wanted attention, her plan had worked. One of the journalists had broken free from the crowd and was now at the side of the stage, holding up a microphone.

"Lady Mayor, surely you and Ms Goremain wouldn't take part in the tasting if one of you had an allergy?"

Zaiba's ears pricked up. The journalist had a point. A head teacher with a serious food allergy wouldn't risk judging a baking competition at a school fete, whether she was new or not. But the Lady Mayor continued wringing her hands, ignoring the journalist. Clearly he wasn't asking her the right questions.

"*Never* in my thirty years of judging this contest has something like this happened."

"I don't understand," Poppy said. "What's she doing?"

Zaiba understood all right. "She's making it all about her," she told Poppy.

Poppy nodded her head wisely. "Ah. Attention-seeking."

Zaiba peered back at Ms Goremain and noticed that the blood had drained from the head teacher's face. Miss Grey was doing her best, but she wasn't a qualified—

"Doctor!" Poppy cried. "A doctor's arrived!" She

pointed to a figure bustling towards the tent with a backpack of supplies and a stethoscope around her neck. A paramedic who looked awfully familiar with her ruby-red smile and glossy hair tied up in a high ponytail.

"Sam!" Zaiba and Poppy cheered. The two of them shared a high five as Samirah (Sam for short) strode into the tent. She was Zaiba's older cousin and a newly qualified doctor. She and Poppy had been to her Mehndi party at a fancy old hotel a few months ago and it was there that they had solved their first official mystery! But there was no glitz and glamour now – Sam had swapped her sari for a medic's uniform and was hurrying over to Ms Goremain to try to find her pulse.

Zaiba felt a rush of pride for her cousin. She'd never seen her in work mode before and it was *very* impressive. Everyone had stepped back for her – even the journalists. Now she kneeled on the stage, shouldering off her backpack to retrieve pieces of equipment at lightning speed. She took out a thermometer and gently placed it in the head teacher's ear, then took her blood pressure with a band wrapped round her arm. With each test, Sam's frown deepened. It was obvious something wasn't right.

The tent was nearly clear of people and Zaiba knew that she and Poppy would be asked to move on at any minute. As they turned to leave, Sam was helping Ms Goremain up.

"We'll take you to your office where I can examine you properly," she said. "No one else should disturb us, thank you."

As Sam helped the head teacher to her feet, she spotted Zaiba at the back of the tent. Their eyes met and Sam shook her head very slightly, as though she guessed the question running round inside Zaiba's head: *Was this an accident?* Sam gave her a look that said, "Something fishy is going on." Then she led Ms Goremain down the steps from the stage and out of a flap at the back of the tent.

As soon as they were outside, Zaiba pulled Poppy aside and looked at her intently. "I don't think this was an allergic reaction," she said, looking around to check no one was listening. "I think The Snow Leopard Detective Agency UK might have its first proper case."

Poppy frowned. "But if it wasn't an allergic reaction, then what could it have been?"

"Did you spot what our new head teacher was holding, when she began choking?"

Poppy bit her lip, thinking. "A flower?"

"It was a cupcake!" Zaiba took a deep breath. "She must have ingested something – something really bad."

Poppy's eyes bulged. "You don't think it was..."

Zaiba turned to the stage, her senses tingling. "That's right, Poppy." She checked over her shoulder that no one could hear her and whispered the last word, "Poison!"

7
CRAFTING A CRIME

Outside the baking tent, it was chaos.

Parents rushed from stand to stand, trying to find out whatever information they could. Was it still safe for them to be there? What had happened to Ms Goremain? Zaiba even overheard one man saying that she was being airlifted to hospital.

"For goodness' sake," Zaiba complained to Poppy as they hurried to the school hall. "The grown-ups are making everything worse."

Some of the kids were totally taking advantage of the unexpected chaos. As they passed the coconut shy, Zaiba saw one boy ignore the three throws only rule, decimating a whole row of coconuts.

"People get out of control when there's a mystery at large," Zaiba told Poppy wisely. "It's important that we keep calm."

"*Keep* calm?" Poppy said. "I'm not sure we've ever *been* calm, Zaiba."

Zaiba chose to ignore her friend's latest observation. They quietly but quickly crossed to the school hall.

Inside the hall, the baking contestants were waiting around under the watch of staff members. She saw Mariam and Raim standing stiffly by the water cooler, avoiding eye contact with each other and everyone else. Next to them, Marco was pacing up and down, clearly still furious that his chance at winning had been sabotaged. Gabriele sat next to him, looking relieved to finally be out of the tent. Hassan and Ali were sitting on one of the fold-out tables the children used for lunch, deep in conversation.

Aha! Zaiba motioned over to Ali – exactly the person she wanted to talk to.

He broke off from talking to Hassan and caught

her eye. "Zaiba!" Her little brother rushed over, his cuffs covered in melted chocolate from the decorating.

As he joined them, Zaiba dragged him over to a corner of the hall. "What did you see?" she urged in a low voice. She got out her Eden Lockett detective notebook and began jotting things down. "I can't believe I wasn't there to witness the crime!"

"So you do think it was a crime?" Ali asked gravely.

"Definitely."

"There's a rumour spreading that Ms Goremain is allergic to nuts. Any info on that?" Poppy pressed. The perfect question! Zaiba was proud of her co-detective.

"That's incorrect." Ali shook his head. "We were given the dietary requirements of each judge before the contest started. It only said that the Lady Mayor was vegetarian."

Zaiba clicked her fingers and jotted that down.

"By the way, did you know that fifteen per cent of food allergies are first diagnosed in adulthood?" Ali tapped on Zaiba's notepad for her to write it down. Ali, the fact master, had struck again. What if the head teacher was reacting to something for the first time?

"I feel sorry for anyone who can't try a honey roasted cashew..." Poppy shook her head.

"Maybe Ms Goremain didn't *know* she couldn't eat certain foods." Zaiba pushed Ali's hand away gently. "I need a clearer picture of the moment the crime took place. Can you describe it?"

Ali paused. "No."

Poppy sighed dramatically.

"But I can show you!" Ali beamed. "I was taking pictures when the tasting was happening."

"Perfect. Pull up the images." Zaiba moved the trio over to a bench where she and Poppy leaned over Ali's shoulder as he flicked through the photos on his new camera, zooming in for details.

"There!" Zaiba pointed to the screen on the third picture Ali showed them.

The judges were on the small stage doing the blind testing, which meant that each contestant's batch of cupcakes was laid out on a countertop. To make sure it was fair they had tied a silk scarf round the judges' eyes and the compere handed them the cupcakes from the plates in front of them. That way they could be sure that the judges weren't playing favourites with the contestants. It really was a serious competition!

In the picture, the three judges each held a cupcake to their mouth. Zaiba did her best to write down any key facts from the photo in her notes.

"OK, so all of the cakes on the plate have had a bite taken out of them – the cakes in their hands are from the last batch. Thomas Hanlon is mid chew, the Lady Mayor has taken a small bite and Ms Goremain has bitten off half ... She must have been hungry." Zaiba noted down every detail, from the people who were standing closest to the judges to the placement of the knives on the countertops. The cakes the judges were tasting in the photo were particularly shiny with different flower petals crystallized on the top.

"Ooh, I would have chosen the rose one." Poppy pointed.

"The atmosphere was tense," Ali whispered. "Auntie Raim was gripping Mariam really tightly, that guy Marco gasped and Dad was doing that annoying tapping thing with his foot. Honestly, you'd think someone was trying to defuse a bomb!"

Zaiba clicked her pen against the paper and thought hard. What they really needed to do first was confirm what had happened to Ms Goremain. She was tucked away inside her office behind a door at the back of the school hall. She looked across the busy hall to locate the doorway only to see Peter, the caretaker, was guarding it. He was taking his job very seriously, blocking any nosy journalists or parents from going through and disturbing the poorly head teacher.

"We need to get through that door. But how?"

Zaiba's brain began whirring. *What would Eden Lockett do?* She instantly thought back to chapter three of *The Flower Show Felony* and it clicked.

She turned to Poppy. "When Eden has to get past the guard to the tool shed at the flower show, what does she do?" Zaiba and Poppy often quizzed each other on Lockett facts. It helped them stay on their toes and keep their minds in detective mode!

"Hmmm." Poppy chewed her lip. "Oh! She throws a

pebble at the greenhouse window, so the guard goes to investigate the noise."

"You want us to smash a window?" Ali didn't look too impressed.

Zaiba shook her head and began eagerly scanning the room "No! I'm saying we need a *distraction*. Let's see if we can find something!"

Poppy and Ali joined Zaiba in her search round the hall for something that could distract the caretaker, but nothing was immediately obvious. To make matters more difficult, the hall was full of witnesses who could ruin their plans. They'd have to be really discreet if they were going to make this work. Then Zaiba noticed the walkie-talkie on Peter's belt, clipped on next to his keys.

"Look!" Poppy said, pointing. "He's got the same walkie-talkie as the people in the sign-up tent."

"I know!" Zaiba gasped. "And look – there's something else." Her gaze dropped to his shoes. They were covered in bits of turf still stuck there from where he'd kicked the grass earlier.

"Oh, wow." Poppy had seen where she was looking.

"That's from when we saw—"

"Exactly!" Zaiba whispered, her eyes glittering. "Come on!"

They ran out to the playground and over to the storage unit at the edge of the green. Just as Zaiba and Poppy had thought! The hole in the turf was still there, right beside the unit's door. Thank goodness the two of them had been alert and in detective mode – you never know what might come in handy!

"Give me your camera." She held out her hand to Ali while checking to make sure they weren't being watched.

"Do I have to?" Ali clutched his precious camera to his chest.

Zaiba blinked. "Do you want Dad to be arrested as a suspect?"

Reluctantly Ali handed over the camera. Zaiba immediately bent down and slid it through the gap created under the base of the unit's door. It disappeared into the storage space and she straightened up, wiping her hands clean with satisfaction.

Ali wasn't so happy. "Hey! That's new!" he protested

but Zaiba shushed him. They couldn't draw attention to what they were doing.

"Trust Zaiba." Poppy wagged her finger at Ali, though she looked a little confused herself.

Zaiba rushed up to one of the receptionists manning the sign-up tent.

"Excuse me, could you help? My little brother's camera got kicked under the door of that storage unit and it's locked!"

The receptionist sighed and picked up her glasses to have a good look at them.

"Honestly, how do you kids get into such messes?"

Zaiba watched as she reached down to the belt of her trousers where she had her walkie-talkie.

The receptionist punched a few numbers into the keypad and held it to her mouth. "Karen to Peter, Karen to Peter..."

There was a moment of static noise before a beep and—

"Peter receiving."

"I need you to come and open that storage unit by the

green. A student's lost their camera in there."

"Uhhhh, I'm in the middle of something important at the moment, can it wait?"

Zaiba rolled her eyes. Peter was taking his security guard job way too seriously.

"I'm sure the head teacher will be fine unguarded for five minutes, Pete."

There was another pause of static buzzing before Peter came back. "Oh, all right. But I'll have to be quick."

Ali grinned at Zaiba, realizing what her plan was, and as soon as the walkie-talkie clicked off Zaiba kicked into action.

"We need to go to the toilet," she told the receptionist. "When Peter has found the camera can you keep it safe for us? Thank you!" She pulled Poppy and Ali off after her before the receptionist could say anything, and they ran back round to the school hall to wait by a set of doors. Within a few seconds Zaiba heard the jangling of keys approaching and Peter trudged through the exit, muttering under his breath. Zaiba let him pass, then signalled for Poppy and Ali to follow her.

They walked quietly yet swiftly towards the now unguarded door that led to the Ms Goremain's office and Zaiba ushered her friends through.

Result! They were in the little waiting area outside the head teacher's office. There were a few chairs where students usually sat and a desk where Ms Goremain's assistant worked. To the right was the deputy head's office, which Zaiba noticed was very small. It wasn't much bigger than a cupboard.

"Let's crouch by that desk," Zaiba whispered, making herself as small as possible and crawling in beside the desk drawers. Poppy and Ali followed her, each of them peering out from beneath a desk leg. Ali's fringe had flopped back down in front of his face and he was trying in vain to push it away. It was pretty tight under there and their knees were up beside their ears.

"This isn't comfortable," Poppy complained.

"It's not meant to be!" Zaiba said, angling her head out from beneath the desk. "Do you think Aunt Fouzia rescued the prime minister of Pakistan by sitting drinking chai?"

Before Poppy could reply, they heard voices emerging from the office and froze.

"Sit still as I take a blood test." Zaiba recognized Sam's voice. "It will only feel like a small prick."

"But what is *he* doing in here?" came the croaky voice of Ms Goremain from inside her office. He? Who else was in there?

"I was just, uh ... checking everything was OK," a deeper voice replied.

Zaiba held her finger to her lips and crawled out from under the desk. She needed to get closer to have a better idea of what was going on inside the office ... and who else was with them. Sam had insisted it should only be her and Ms Goremain!

"And I was also ... calling the police chief!" the voice continued. It sounded familiar.

Oh no, Zaiba thought. In the village where they lived crimes were rare – Zaiba knew all too well what this meant. Their local police chief was known for sensing trouble where there wasn't any. If he ever did get his hands on a real crime his imagination often got the better of him! Once Jessica had reported her handbag missing, only to have the police chief launch a district-wide investigation into a handbag-stealing gang that never existed. If he came to the fete, the crime – if one had actually been committed – would never get solved. Or worse, the wrong person would be arrested.

"I never asked for that. I think you should leave!" Ms Goremain replied. She sounded very upset and Zaiba felt a pang of sadness for her. This was her first summer fete as head teacher and it had been ruined. The door handle to the office started to rattle and Poppy's head swung to Zaiba, her eyes wide. *They were about to be found out!*

Quick! They needed an escape!

Looking about her, Zaiba's eyes settled on the crafts cupboard near the assistant's desk. She beckoned Poppy and Ali to follow and ran over, keeping low, to swing the cupboard door open. Thank goodness it was unlocked! No one seemed to think that bags of wool and boxes of felt and embroidery thread were worth keeping safe. All three began ruffling about inside, pretending to collect supplies and hoping that whoever it was would pass them by.

Zaiba picked up a large piece of tin foil – some sort of metallic cardboard – and angled it to peer at the reflection. Eden Lockett said that: *Mirrors come in useful in all sorts of ways.* As the light caught the foil, she saw the reflection. Someone was skulking out of the head teacher's office, his face like thunder.

Thomas Hanlon – the school governor!

As the door was shut in his face and he was left in the waiting area, he shook his head. "If only she'd listened to at least *one* of the points in my School Fete Suggestions Pack. Page fifty *clearly* states to have the police on standby."

Zaiba was pretty sure they must have been the most boring fifty pages ever written. She could just imagine it – page thirty-five, how to stop a squirrel climbing a school tree!

But as Thomas Hanlon turned to leave, the craft cupboard door swung open with a creak of hinges and he immediately spotted the friends hiding.

"What are you doing here?" he growled.

Zaiba, Poppy and Ali looked at each other, mouths open. *Uh-oh* ... They needed to think up a craft-related excuse quickly!

"We were looking for some crepe paper—" Zaiba began, only to be saved by Ms Goremain's office door being thrown open. There was Sam standing in the doorway. She was facing away from them, but they could see she was holding an electrical device with figures showing on its digital monitor. Zaiba noticed a small white tab at the bottom stained red with blood. It was a blood-test machine!

"I'm not sure," Sam was saying. "I could be wrong ..."

She shook the device and stared at the results screen once more.

Ms Goremain's voice called from inside her office. She sounded strained and worried. "What do you mean it might be poison?"

8
POISONOUS RUMOURS

At the sound of the word *poison*! Thomas Hanlon's eyes bulged. Then he strode out into the school hall, moving as fast as he could. He seemed to have forgotten all about Zaiba, Poppy and Ali trespassing.

As soon as he disappeared from sight, Zaiba scrambled away from the cupboard and ran over to the office door. Sam was emerging from the room and Zaiba went to squeeze her free hand. The other was still gripping the blood-test machine tightly.

"Are you OK?" Zaiba whispered. Sam nodded and quietly shut the door behind her.

Sam glanced through into the school hall, where

Thomas Hanlon had rushed after hearing her discovery. "Go after him. Don't let him spread any rumours."

"But was she poisoned?" Poppy looked worriedly at Sam. Although Ms Goremain could be strict, they definitely didn't want her to be ill.

"Yes but only enough to cause dizziness and vomiting. With some rest she'll be fine. Thankfully she doesn't need to go to hospital." Sam smiled at Poppy to reassure her and Zaiba felt even prouder of her cousin. She was turning out to be an amazing doctor! Zaiba could only hope she'd be as good a detective.

"Any idea of the substance used to poison her?" Ali asked in a low voice. "Arsenic? Morphine?"

Zaiba stared at her little brother. "What have you been reading? Agatha Christie?"

Ali shrugged. "Dad liked to have crime movies playing on the laptop when we practised our baking."

Sam shook her head, laughing gently. "Nothing as bad as that. I need to send the results to the hospital but any news I'll let you know. For now, can you follow Hanlon and stop him before he tells everyone Celia has exploded or something equally ridiculous. We can't have any false information flying around, especially if the police chief is on his way... Hanlon shouldn't have been in the head's office at all." Her face turned dark. "I can't stand busybodies."

Sam is in the wrong place, Zaiba thought. *The school seems to be full of them!* Zaiba gave her cousin one last hug. "You can rely on us."

Sam's eyes glinted. "I know. Off you go – quick!" They made their way back into the school hall, hot on Thomas Hanlon's trail. As the police had been called, they were on a countdown to solve the crime before the chief turned up and blew everything out of proportion.

Peter had returned to his post and his eyes bugged when he saw *three more people* coming out of the offices he was supposed to be guarding. "What were you doing in there?"

But Zaiba kept her head down and kept moving. Where had the school governor gone?

"Of course, this would *never* have happened on my

watch..." A voice boomed from over by the lemonade table. Zaiba's eyes narrowed. *Hanlon.*

They marched up to him as he continued gloating to a group of parents and teachers. "But she's very new and she *hadn't* read my School Fete Suggestions Pack, which would have prevented this from happening."

"Excuse me," Zaiba said, tapping him on the back. "I think there must be some mistake."

Hanlon spun round, clearly irritated at having his speech interrupted. "Little girls shouldn't interfere where they're not—"

"Us interfere?!" Poppy exploded, pointing a quivering finger at Hanlon. "But you're the person sticking his nose in where it's not wanted!"

There was a collective gasp from the parents. They weren't used to children speaking to grown-ups in this way and it was too late to explain that, actually, Poppy was right. Zaiba linked her arm with her friend's as the parents gathered round them.

"You can't speak to a school governor like that!" Hanlon tapped his name badge.

"I've never heard such a thing!" said one of the parents. "This is what social media does to children! Really, young lady, you should apologize!"

"I don't even use social media," Poppy grumbled. "Well, only when it's something special, like when Maysoon announces a new film."

Zaiba noticed that Mariam was watching darkly from a small distance away. Why was she always around when there was trouble brewing? Zaiba's arm tightened round Poppy's. "Maybe it's best to apologize," she whispered. "It will save us some time."

The heel of Poppy's boots scuffed against the hall tiles as she stared sulkily at her feet. "I am very ... sorry," she squeezed out.

"Very sorry, Mr Hanlon," the school governor prompted.

"Sorry, Mr Hanlon," Poppy repeated, her cheeks flaming.

But it was still too late – Zaiba could see that word about the poisoning was spreading. Grown-ups had gathered in clusters and one of the parents was moving from group to group, her arms waving around and her hands clutching her throat. Zaiba could almost see the word – *POISON!* – floating in the air above everyone's heads.

Honestly, she thought. *Don't they have anything better to talk about? Usually all they talked about was parking permits and new bathrooms!*

As Zaiba scanned the school hall she caught snippets of conversations.

"I heard the head's been unconscious for hours!"

"Thomas Hanlon said she rejected his help. She wanted to do the fete by herself."

"All the food here is contaminated. Who knows where the poison came from?"

More people were filing into the school hall from outside on the village green, including Jessica, who immediately went to console Hassan. Most of the crowd were eager to get more information and stay as far away from the baking tent as possible.

"Zaiba, what about the detective trail contestants?" Poppy suddenly remembered. She looked at her pink diamante watch. "They should be going to find the clue in the library now."

"Never mind that. We need to solve the crime!" Ali protested.

Zaiba looked from her best friend to her brother. They were both right. She paused and cleared her head. What would Eden Lockett do?

"I guess we'll have to do both." She set her sights on the hallway that led up to the school library. "Let's go!"

As they moved through the crowd, they passed the baking contestants. Marco was ranting at Hassan, jabbing his finger at the wooden plaque on the wall.

"Second ... second ... SECOND!" he yelled over and over. "This year was supposed to be my chance to come FIRST! But no, all my hard work has been ruined."

Hassan winced and tried to pat Marco on the back. "Come on, it's OK. This is supposed to be a fun family contest, remember?"

But Marco shrugged off Hassan's hand. He didn't want to be comforted.

Hassan caught Zaiba's eye and waved her over.

"Do you know anything, Zaiba? Is ... is it true?" he asked, a little shakily. "I heard the rumours about poison." He placed a hand on her shoulder. "Are you going to be doing any detective work on this?"

Zaiba felt a flush of pride as her dad looked at her hopefully. *Wow, he really must have faith in me*.

She put on her best Serious Detective face. "It's true. But Sam says the poison isn't enough to do any damage. Ms Goremain will be fine. We just need to find out who did this."

It occurred to her that although the list of suspects would include anyone who had access to the cupcakes, she would have to closely investigate each baker in the competition – including her dad! His eyes crinkled with anxiety. He must have realized that too.

First things first though, she needed to check on her detective trail contestants. They were still looking for clues. Zaiba should let them know that the trail hunt might be temporarily suspended – after all, she would have her hands full with solving the poisoning! She reached up on tiptoe to kiss her dad's cheek and turned to leave. She noticed Marco was watching her, his eyes narrowed.

Had she said something wrong? Why was he glaring at her? But before Zaiba could even try to give him a smile, Marco turned his back on her and returned to scowling at the wooden plaque on the wall.

Zaiba could almost feel his burning stare scorching into the names on the board.

He *really* needed to get over that.

9
TWO NEW RECRUITS

Zaiba stepped inside the cool of the library to find
her teams of detectives furiously hunting through
bookshelves and under tables. One team, dressed
in Hawaiian shirts and long black wigs, had taken to
removing all the books from the shelves one by one.
Another team was dressed as mimes – complete with
black and white face paint. They were busy checking
inside each book, flipping through the pages and
shaking them to see if any clue fell out. A final team
was carefully replacing each book back on its shelf after
they'd searched it for clues.

Teamwork, I like it! Zaiba mentally gave them bonus

points for being thorough. The contestants were all so engrossed in their detective work that they didn't even notice Zaiba, Poppy and Ali walking down an aisle.

Zaiba counted heads. It looked as though four contestants hadn't reached the library yet. Had she made the trail too hard? But there wasn't time to worry about that now.

"Hi, everyone! If you could stop what you're doing for a minute," Zaiba called out. The shuffling and rushing around slowly died down and they turned their attention to Zaiba. The library was a large square room, with one corner dedicated to an IT suite and the remaining space lined with huge floor-to-ceiling bookshelves. To ensure everyone could see her, Zaiba took up position in front of the librarian's desk at the top of the room.

She cleared her throat. "I'm afraid there's been an incident with the head teacher and the trail is, uh ... on pause." She didn't want to concern the detectives by using words like 'poison' and certainly not 'cancelled'.

"Maybe you can finish the trail another time?" Poppy offered, noting the disappointed looks on the contestant's faces.

"Aren't you meant to be dead?" one of them asked.

Ah yes, Poppy had forgotten about that. She still had a few smears of fake blood left on her face and arms. "Erm, that was, I mean..." Her voice trailed to a halt.

"That was pretend," Ali finished for her. "Poppy was just acting!"

"Not *just* acting," Poppy protested, pulling her shoulders back. "I worked really hard to make my performance perfect!"

A contestant in a Sherlock Holmes cap rolled his eyes. "We know you weren't really dead! We just wanted to win the prize. But a real-life crime? That's much more interesting!"

Zaiba held a hand up to stop any further conversation. "Only professionals can investigate this case." She gave the group a warning look. "Amateur detecting could prove disastrous. And *dangerous*."

There was a moment of silence before a little boy – the one who'd seemed particularly queasy over Poppy's murder – piped up. "Can we at least finish the detective trail?" He had a steely look of determination and Poppy positively beamed – her dramatic performance had paid off!

Zaiba looked to Poppy and shrugged. "OK then! We wanted to keep you informed. Carry on, but just be aware that we may not be around to judge the teams. Not until this new case is solved!"

As soon as the words left her mouth, the contestants were off again, running round the room, pushing chairs aside and digging through boxes of books. Zaiba realized the librarian might not be too happy with her when she came in on Monday morning ... but she would deal with that then. Right now she had to find out who had poisoned the head teacher – and why!

Turning to leave, Zaiba suddenly noticed Ali wasn't beside them any more. He was sitting over in the IT suite, staring hard at the screen on one of the computers.

"Oh, for goodness' sake, Ali." She sighed, going over to drag him away. "Are you playing games again? We have a crime to solve!"

"I know!" Ali protested. He pointed at the screen,

where Zaiba could see rolling headlines on the kids' news channel. "I'm checking out the latest news. Look!"

Zaiba came to peer over his shoulder at the article he was reading, *Cake Crime at School Fete!* She groaned. "Listen to this, 'The head teacher may only be the first of many victims. Who knows when this poison plot will be uncovered?'"

"That's going to be make everyone panic!" Poppy gasped.

Zaiba nodded. "That's why we've got to solve this mystery quickly."

"Can we help?" came a voice from under the desk.

Poppy yelped. "Who was that?" she gasped, bending down to peer under the desk. Then two little heads popped out.

It was Mariam and Gabriele!

"What are you doing here?" Zaiba gasped. "You're supposed to be in the hall with the other bakers."

Gabriele's lip trembled. "We're hiding. This whole thing is too stressful, especially with our parents acting like they are."

Strangely, Mariam's face looked a bit wobbly too. Zaiba realized she had never seen her cousin look frightened before. Mariam came out from beneath the desk and pleaded with Zaiba in a small voice.

"Zaiba, I know my mum is one of the suspects because she was a baker. But she would never try to murder anyone – believe me! We have to prove she's innocent."

"First of all, this isn't a murder case." Zaiba folded her arms. "The poison was only enough to cause dizziness and vomiting."

"You don't know, Zai." Poppy shook her head. "The criminal might get cocky. It could be poison today, murder tomorrow. Do you want to risk that?"

Zaiba had to admit she didn't. "No. And we have to consider each suspect equally." Of course they wanted their parents to be innocent, but someone had to be guilty. Mariam's words made her think back to her conversation with Hassan. Did Zaiba have to treat him like a suspect as well as the others? She decided it was down to her detective honour to do just that. *My dad, a suspect?* She'd never considered this when she set up the UK branch of the Snow Leopard Detective Agency!

"Ugh, fine." Mariam pouted. "I knew you wouldn't understand." She folded her arms across her chest and plonked herself down on a library chair.

Zaiba *did* understand. That was the whole problem. But how could she explain to Mariam – or anyone for that matter? She was starting to understand that being a detective could be lonely work. She really enjoyed piecing together the clues with her friends, but as head of the Snow Leopard Detective Agency UK she was the only person who could point an accusing finger at someone. She had to take on board everyone's thoughts and then decide – who was the guilty suspect? These were hard decisions to make. She was beginning to realize how strong and brave Aunt Fouzia was.

"I want to get away from my dad," Gabriele said, pulling himself up from under the desk. "Baking was supposed to be about us bonding but he wouldn't even let me try the cupcakes! I'm sick of this stupid competition." Gabriele's curly black hair flopped in front of his face. Zaiba noticed Ali looking at it enviously. If Ali had a curly fringe he could grow it even longer!

"Can't the Snow Leopard Detective Agency take two more recruits?" Gabriele asked.

"The Snow Leopard Detective Agency *UK*," Zaiba corrected. "Anyway, how do you know about that?"

Mariam's face blushed. "Er, I told him."

Zaiba shook her head. "So much for discretion." What kind of detective could Mariam possibly make anyway? But she felt herself melting. She remembered how lonely and sad her cousin had looked back at the Royal Star Hotel when she'd been on her own. Was this Zaiba's chance to let Mariam feel part of something?

"Right, sorry." Gabriele nodded. "Well?"

Zaiba looked over at Mariam and raised her eyebrows.

"I wouldn't normally want to be part of your little detective games ... but I need to prove my mum is innocent!"

Zaiba could hardly believe it. Would Mariam ever get the hang of being friendly?

"What makes you think you would be a good

detective?" Zaiba folded her arms, pressing Mariam for an answer.

"*Phsst*," Mariam scoffed. "Don't you remember *I* was the one who found out it was Grandpa stealing all the luddu at our last Eid party?"

Zaiba turned red. She'd forgotten Mariam had solved that mystery. But really the whole family had suspected their greedy Grandpa was the culprit.

"Oh! Oh! And I'm very observant and curious," Gabriele jumped up and down. "I think those are good qualities for a detective."

Zaiba's heart melted even further.

"Give me a moment," she said. "I need to discuss this with my team. Agents, assemble!" She motioned to Poppy and Ali and they scurried behind a bookshelf.

They had an important decision to make. *Should the Snow Leopard Detective Agency UK recruit Mariam and Gabriele?*

"Will this take long, do you think?" Zaiba heard Gabriele whisper.

Mariam let out a long sigh. "Probably! Knowing Zaiba,

she's drawing up a list and checking it twice. She likes that kind of thing."

It was true! Zaiba had already pulled her Eden Lockett notebook out of her bag. She drew a long line down the middle of the page. In the left hand column, she wrote 'PROS' and in the right hand column 'CONS'.

"Right, meeting commenced," Zaiba whispered. "Ali, you first. I'll take notes."

Ali screwed up his nose and thought hard.

"I don't trust Mariam as much as you." He looked at Zaiba. "Remember when she popped all the clown's balloons at your birthday party once because she said balloon animals are for babies?"

Zaiba nodded. She would never forget. The fact that Zaiba and Mariam always had to share a birthday party only made their rivalry worse.

"But then again," Ali continued. "Having two more people on the team increases the probability of us solving the case."

Zaiba smiled and scribbled that down in the PROS column.

Now it was Poppy's turn to say her piece. "I definitely feel sorry for Gabriele. It can't be fun having such a competitive dad and it *would* be handy to have insider knowledge from the competition. Other than Ali, of course."

Zaiba hurriedly wrote down Poppy's points. The page was soon filling up with details.

"BUT." Poppy tapped the page. "Make sure you note down that Mariam's wearing jelly shoes. That might slow her down – everyone knows your feet get sweaty and slippy in jellies..."

Zaiba and Ali giggled, but she wrote it down nonetheless.

They studied the columns. There was an equal amount of pros and cons. It was up to Zaiba to make the final decision. She looked over the list once more then slowly walked out from behind the bookshelf.

"Mariam? Gabriele?"

Gabriele rushed over to Zaiba with Mariam close behind.

Zaiba looked from one face to the other. She could

see cake crumbs, sweat ... and hope. She gave them an encouraging smile. "I've decided to recruit you to the Snow Leopard Detective Agency UK!" Gabriele let out a cheer and hugged Mariam, jumping up and down on the spot. Even Mariam let herself smile a little. "On a temporary basis only." Zaiba held out her hand to shake. Mariam reached out and shook it while Gabriele went straight in for a massive hug. Carefully Zaiba peeled herself free. "Now, first we need a mission briefing."

They huddled together and Zaiba took a deep breath. "Right team, here's the plan. Ali and Gabriele will head down to the school hall to observe the bakers and report back. Try and find out some information about that compere, he was handling the cupcakes too. Oh, and Ali, remember to collect your camera in case you need to photograph any evidence. Also, we have to remember – our parents are potential suspects."

"Not mine!" Poppy added.

"Not yours, but we need to keep an open mind. See what you can find out. All information is useful."

"You've got it." Ali nodded.

"I'll do my best!" Gabriele agreed.

"Meanwhile Poppy, Mariam and I will scout the village green, starting with the baking tent. There must be some evidence left lying around. It's like Aunt Fouzia always says to me, 'Where there's a crime, there's a trail'." She thought about some of the other classrooms. "We should check out the science lab at some point too. If the poison was prepared in the school, that would be a good place to do it!"

"Well, obviously," Mariam scoffed.

Zaiba ignored her. Now that they had a plan, nothing could hold her back. Her eyes sparkled. This was what she was born to do! She held up a palm and they all high-fived as best they could – although it wasn't easy when there was an odd number of detectives. Ali accidentally high-fived Gabriele in the face but he didn't seem to mind.

"Agents!" she cried. "Let's solve this crime!"

10
THE BITTER TASTE OF REVENGE

How does a detective gather evidence without touching anything? Zaiba's mind whirled through the details of this dilemma as she headed out on to the village green.

A small crowd of people were still milling about, despite the rumours of poisoning. They gathered round the various stands, playing Hook a Duck or trying their luck at the Tombola, but Zaiba noticed a big, empty space around the baking tent.

No one wanted to be near the scene of the crime. No one but Zaiba and her team.

She led the way to the tent, Poppy and Mariam in tow.

"We have to uncover the motive for poisoning the cupcakes, and it might be helpful to know who made the cupcakes in question," she thought out loud. Her mind scrolled back through all the Eden Lockett novels she'd read and the motivations for crime. There had been *The Secret of the Forgotten Necklace*, where someone had taken revenge for a piece of jewellery they hadn't inherited, *The Mystery of the Deep Lake*, where a boat owner had had an argument with the head gardener and *The Clown's Clue* where a spiteful circus performer had ruined his competitor's trapeze act. What did they all have in common?

Revenge.

Zaiba looked round the village green. "We need to think about who here could be holding a secret, or not so secret, grudge. Who in the competition didn't look happy."

"Also shouldn't the police be here? Mr Hanlon had said he was calling the chief," Poppy asked. That had been over fifteen minutes ago and everyone knew how eager the police chief was to solve a crime. This would be his dream come true!

"Hopefully he's been distracted by something. For now, *we're* in charge of this investigation." Zaiba caught Mariam's eye and forced an encouraging smile. This was Mariam's first case and it could be quite overwhelming for a trainee detective – especially one with a bad attitude.

As they approached the baking tent a familiar figure came into view, standing outside the entrance.

"Oh, for goodness' sake! He's everywhere!" Zaiba sighed as she watched Peter turn away a parent. "Hold on – look!"

Mr Hanlon was striding over to the tent, panting. The school governor must have finally taken a break from spreading rumours! He jerked his thumb over his shoulder towards the rose garden. "One of the goats from the petting zoo has got loose in your rose garden. We can't catch it!" he told Peter.

"Not my roses!" The caretaker immediately took off across the green and Mr Hanlon ran after him.

"He *really* loves those roses..." Mariam muttered,

making Poppy giggle.

Now was their chance. They rushed over to the baking tent and with one last check around them, dived inside.

It certainly looked like a crime scene, with everything left exactly as it had been the minute Ms Goremain fell ill. Plates and cups had been dropped on the spot, fans were still whirring, chairs were strewn around and there, sitting on the counter at the front of the tent, were the cupcakes.

"Search the tent thoroughly," Zaiba instructed. "Note anything suspicious but *do not touch*!"

As Poppy and Mariam searched the perimeters Zaiba cautiously approached the cupcakes. She got out her phone recorder to take notes.

"The time is 14:30, we have entered the crime scene. On the countertop are three plates. Each plate has three cupcakes – one from each contestant. All cupcakes have had a bite taken out of them. Since we don't know what the poison is or how long it takes to have an effect, all the cupcakes Ms Goremain tasted are under suspicion."

Zaiba momentarily covered the recorder and beckoned Mariam over. "Which cupcakes were yours?"

Mariam pointed to a plate and Zaiba resumed her recording.

"Mariam and Aunt Raim's cupcakes were decorated with gold icing and red sprinkles. Ali and Dad's cupcakes were decorated with edible henna patterns."

"The best in my opinion," Poppy added, coming to peer over Zaiba's shoulder. This prompted a scowl from Mariam, which Zaiba ignored.

"That leaves the cupcakes decorated with different types of edible flower petals, which must be Gabriele and Marco's. They are the ones the judges tasted last. The petals are rose, violet and ..." Zaiba leaned in close to the little descriptive sign in front of the cupcakes, "nasturtium. Note for Agent Zaiba to ask Mum what nasturtium is. Agents will confer over possible suspects." Zaiba clicked off her phone recorder.

"Possible suspects... You mean our parents?" Mariam said shakily.

Zaiba was surprised. Mariam's mum was so strict yet

Mariam seemed to really care about clearing her name.

"I—I—I don't want my mum to go to prison!" Mariam suddenly cried out and burst into tears. Poppy and Zaiba were rooted to the spot—they had never *ever* seen Mariam weeping! "She hates it when we're apart and if she went to prison we'd be separated for—for—for ever!" Mariam was really bawling and Zaiba was concerned her noisy tears would attract unwanted attention.

"It's OK, Mariam. Don't worry." Zaiba patted her on the back. "We won't let your mum go to prison." *Or my dad for that matter*, she thought to herself. "We have to get to bottom of this before the police chief turns up. It's the only way to clear our parents' names!"

After a few final sobs, Mariam took a deep breath and let her shoulders slump. She nodded ever so slightly and wiped her nose with a spare serviette. "You're right. We'll solve the crime to protect our parents. Even if it means we have to investigate them."

"It's not just the bakers who could have slipped poison into the cupcakes," Zaiba pointed out. "There are plenty of other people who could have used the opportunity to hurt Ms Goremain."

Poppy's eyes glistened. "But who would want to hurt her?"

Zaiba flipped open her notebook to a fresh new page. Again she drew a table with two columns – but this time she labelled the left-hand one 'SUSPECTS + MOTIVES' and the right-hand column one 'OPPORTUNITY'.

"Who are you going to start with?" Poppy asked. "Who are the prime suspects?"

Zaiba smiled and began scribbling away. "Let's see..."

SUSPECTS + MOTIVES	OPPORTUNITY
1. **Deputy head, Miss Grey** Wants to be head teacher, angry that Ms Goremain got the promotion instead of her. Immediately took over when Ms Goremain was ill – had been planning for the moment?	She was helping out backstage in the tent. Suspiciously lurking by the fridge. She is a science teacher (has access to poison?).
2. **Peter the caretaker** Protective over crime scene – doesn't want anyone snooping about. Angry with Ms Goremain for not caring about his prize rose garden.	Helped set up the fete. Has keys to every room in the school, including science room (access to chemicals – potential poison?).

"What about Thomas Hanlon?" Poppy's cheeks burned at the memory of her scolding. "He has to be guilty of something!"

Zaiba nodded, remembering how the school governor had been nosing around in Ms Goremain's office — supposedly calling the police. So why wasn't the police chief here already? He could be checking these clues himself! She got back to writing, Poppy's words still ringing in her ears.

3. Thomas Hanlon Angry that Ms Goremain won't listen to his suggestions as school governor. Feels disrespected?	Was also a judge. Could have slipped poison into cupcakes during the tasting.
4. Lady Mayor Wanted all the attention on her for the judging. Didn't like the attention the new head teacher was getting?	Was also a judge. Could have slipped poison into cupcakes during the tasting.

"That's a lot of people. My mind's spinning. They've *all* acted suspiciously and have motives." Poppy rubbed her temples as if she was encouraging her brain to work harder.

"And that's not even including the bakers." Zaiba shook out her achy hand and got ready to start writing again.

As Zaiba wrote down Aunt Raim's name, Mariam whimpered. Zaiba gave her a stern look and Mariam took a deep breath. "OK, go on."

5. Aunt Raim Angry at Ms Goremain for moving Mariam down a set in maths (big argument in playground).	Baked and decorated the cakes.
6. Marco Really competitive, bad loser.	Baked and decorated the cakes.
7. Dad (Hassan) No obvious motive.	Baked and decorated the cakes.

Now Zaiba's hand was *really* aching but luckily they were done. Seven suspects, so far... Some with stronger motives than others.

"Our prime suspects are numbers one to three." Zaiba started off the discussion. "Anyone want to guess why?" It was important that she didn't do all the detective work herself – her co-agents should be as knowledgeable as she was. She remembered Aunt Fouzia's words last time they'd spoken: *A team working together will always get the job done quicker.*

"OK, so," Poppy rubbed her hands together, "even though the Lady Mayor loves the attention, she seemed as surprised as anyone when Ms Goremain got ill. She also doesn't have a strong motive for wanting to poison her."

Zaiba beamed proudly at her second-in-command.

Next Mariam cleared her throat. "And Marco is very competitive, but Ms Goremain is new to the school so I don't see why he'd have anything against her. As for Uncle Hassan and my mum, I don't see a strong motive for either of them either." Mariam leaned back on her heels with a pleased smile.

"Apart from your mum shouting at Ms Goremain in the school playground," Poppy said under her breath.

"She only did that because Ms Goremain was rude!" Mariam countered.

"I'm just saying, it does look a bit fishy that she was *sooooooo* angry with Ms Goremain and then she was poisoned," reasoned Poppy.

Mariam's face coloured. "She was angry because I got moved down a set!"

"Enough!" Zaiba cried. "We can't be a team if we're bickering! There are more important things at hand." Maybe she'd been too naïve to think that there was a friendship brewing between the three of them. But she couldn't let that get in their way!

Zaiba ran her finger over the page once more before snapping the book shut. "Do you know what we have here? A whole load of theory – good ideas but no evidence! Now it's time for action."

"Agreed." Mariam nodded firmly.

"Also agreed!" Poppy added.

"We must have everything clear before the police chief arrives. An overeager police officer can be disastrous for an investigation! I remember Aunt Fouzia told us about a case she was working on at Sukoon Bazaar where the police turned up before she had finished investigating. They ended up arresting the wrong man because one of the officers didn't know the difference between a kaddu and a dudhi!"

"I mean, I don't know what either of those things are," Poppy said.

"They're types of vegetable. What I mean is," Zaiba ploughed on, "the same injustice will not happen here just because the police chief wants to make a name for himself! He's so bored he'd arrest anyone to give him something to do. Whereas we'll get all the evidence straight and catch the real criminal."

The sound of more fete-goers approaching the village green floated in through the walls of the tent. Zaiba could hear their voices getting louder. Some of the parents were complaining that they were missing the football for this! She knew that the more people moved about, the more danger there was of evidence being destroyed. They had to solve this case as quickly as possible!

"I think we should get a move on before someone finds us here," Mariam said, peering out of a flap in the tent. She was getting the hang of this!

"All right, team." Zaiba clapped her hands together. "Let's touch base with Ali and Gabriele. Then we can put our theories to the test!"

11
TROUBLE ON THE DETECTIVE TRAIL

Three heads popped out from the entrance flaps of the baking tent, one on top of the other. Mariam then Zaiba and finally Poppy peered on to the village green waiting for the perfect moment to leave the crime scene undetected.

"We'll be with you soon," Zaiba whispered into her phone, checking in with Ali. "We've just finished investigating the crime scene."

"OK." Ali's voice came back through the phone's speakers. "But hurry up. Tensions are running high in the hall!"

A small group of teachers were still huddled together,

discussing the poisoning. Snippets drifted over towards the friends.

"I've always said that—"

"Health and security risk—"

"Should phone the union and let them know—"

"Postpone return to school—"

"Yes!" Poppy whispered. "More time off school."

"There are more important matters to hand, Poppy! Although an extra long summer holiday would be good..."

The teachers finally cleared off and the trio slipped out – and not a moment too soon. Peter the caretaker was marching back from his rose garden. If he'd found the friends in the baking tent, goodness knows what he'd have done.

"Zaiba, your mum wants us." Poppy pointed in the direction of the face-painting stand, where Jessica was beckoning to them.

The girls rushed over to the shelter of the stand. The sun was blazing and Jessica was trying to keep her paints cool with a fan before they turned into messy puddles.

"Hi, girls, it's nice to see you being friends." Jessica smiled, clearly surprised and pleased to see Mariam as part of the group.

"We're investigating." Zaiba kept her voice low so as not to attract attention.

Jessica's expression suddenly turned serious. "You know I'm very proud of you running the Snow Leopard Detective Agency but—"

"*UK branch*," Zaiba corrected. Details were important!

"Of course, UK branch," Jessica added quickly. "But please be careful. This is a crime scene and the police will need to collect evidence. Especially if that ... *imaginative* police chief is involved." Zaiba thought her stepmum was being quite polite.

"We know, Auntie Jessica. We are being careful. Zaiba told us not to touch anything," Mariam came to Zaiba's defence.

Wow, Mariam was starting to get the hang of being a team player!

"I'm glad to hear it." Jessica dabbed her forehead with a napkin.

A group of boys turned up at the face-painting stand, which meant Jessica had to get back to work. And that was just as well – Zaiba, Mariam and Poppy needed to focus!

Their first point of investigation was the caretaker. He was one of the prime suspects and they needed to do some further digging. But when Zaiba looked over to the baking tent, he was no longer there. "Where's Peter gone? When he's not wanted he's always there and when you need him he's nowhere to be seen!"

The three girls scanned the village green until Zaiba spotted him. "There he is – heading back to the rose garden. AGAIN! Let's follow him. Make sure you keep your distance."

They stalked Peter over to the rose garden, staying ten paces behind him all the way. As they followed, Mariam filled the girls in on some extra information.

"You know, I overheard Ms Goremain talking to the caretaker when she first started. She was asking why the school is in charge of the rose garden, since it's technically off school grounds. The caretaker seemed really angry. He said he'd been looking after it for fifteen years and he doesn't plan to stop now."

They slowly crept up to the trellising on one side of the rose garden and each peeped through one of the little holes.

Zaiba put her eye to the gap and saw Peter bending down near the bushes. She squinted hard.

"I can't see what he's doing!" she whispered. Luckily Poppy was a bit taller.

"It looks like he's cutting the roses and bunching them together. Oh, he's making a bouquet!" she whispered back. "Do you think they're for Ms Goremain? He doesn't seem to like her very much..."

He straightened up and carefully tied the bouquet together with curls of pink ribbon, whistling some sort of romantic tune to himself. Then he turned on his heel and began heading straight towards them.

"Duck! He's coming this way!"

The three of them crouched behind a hedge as Peter made his way out of the garden, holding the bouquet.

Zaiba held up her hand and when the caretaker was far enough ahead she dropped it down, signalling the girls to follow.

Peter strode across the village green and over to the main stage area where the Lady Mayor was still talking to a few people. But rather than going up to her, he stopped a short distance away, staring at her intently.

"Oh, and to think that this is supposed to be a day for *families*, for something so awful to happen..." The Lady Mayor might have been some distance away from Zaiba, Poppy and Mariam, who were now lurking behind the raffle stall, but they could still hear her dramatic wails. The caretaker was going to be waiting a long time if he wanted to talk to the Lady Mayor.

He must have had the same thought, because he discreetly walked over to the Lady Mayor's handbag (not difficult to spot as it matched her dress – green with silk roses) and gently placed the bouquet on top of it. He straightened up, took one last forlorn look at the Lady Mayor and sighed, before heading off towards the school.

"Of course!" Zaiba exclaimed, coming out from behind their hiding place.

"Of course what?" Mariam frowned.

"He hasn't been acting sneakily because he's a suspect, he's been acting sneakily because he has a crush on the Lady Mayor!"

Poppy stuck her tongue out and made a sick face. "Gross! Why do adults have to do that?"

"That's why he was so obsessed with keeping the rose garden nice, because he knows the Lady Mayor loves roses – she's even got them all over her dress."

"And that's why he was so upset when the judges wouldn't come on a tour of the rose garden. He wanted to impress her." Poppy clicked her fingers. It was all falling into place.

Zaiba got out her notebook and crossed off Peter's name from the list of suspects. Being in love did not equal being a poisoner. "We need to move our investigations on to our other suspects. And luckily we know they're in the school hall, where Ali and Gabriele are. Let's go."

As they rushed across the village green, Zaiba retrieved her phone and clicked on the recorder.

"Suspect two, the caretaker, is no longer under investigation. We are moving our enquiry on to suspect one – the deputy head, Miss Grey. Questions with the baking competition finalists to follow."

But before they crossed the road, a pair of contestants from Zaiba's detective trail found her. Oh no! Zaiba had been totally preoccupied with the latest mystery and had forgotten about her gang of budding detectives. The team that had found her was the little boy who had caught the detective bug and his older brother. They ran up to Zaiba and held out their activity sheet.

"Zaiba, we're stuck! We thought we'd found the last clue but something must have gone wrong," said the older brother.

"And we were in the lead!" the little boy pouted.

Zaiba narrowed her eyes. She had checked this trail countless times – nothing could have gone wrong! She hesitated, not wanting to delay her investigations any further. Her auntie and her dad were at risk of falsely being accused of a crime. But then again, she had promised her Aunt Fouzia to uphold the Snow Leopard Detective Agency's reputation and she'd really wanted to create a proper crime trail for the contestants to follow.

"Take me to it," she said, being careful not to give away too much in case they had made a mistake. Zaiba had been meaning to investigate this location anyway... She caught Poppy's eye. Her friend was frowning – something wasn't right.

The two boys led them to the science lab, where the last detective trail clue was indeed hidden. With the medical tests confirming Ms Goremain had been poisoned, the science lab was a key place to search and this was the perfect opportunity. Luckily, the science teacher had given them special access! Earlier, Zaiba had planted a pair of scissors in the lab with fake blood on them – the final clue that this was the murder's weapon. The plan had been that the budding detectives would find the weapon and solve the crime by a process of elimination. The scissors were left-handed, and there was only one suspect who was known to be left-handed! She eagerly followed them to the classroom. But when Zaiba peered into the steel bin where she had hidden the scissors, it was empty!

"See?" the little boy moaned. "There's nothing there!"

Zaiba was gobsmacked. How had it disappeared? The bin was empty apart from some dust, petals and crumbs.

"But we put a sign next to it saying DO NOT MOVE," Poppy exclaimed. "Plus, it's the weekend. No one should be using the science lab..."

Mariam shifted side to side, tapping her fingers on one of the desks. "Zaiba," she whispered. "Do you think this could be a clue for *our* investigation?"

Mariam had a point. Zaiba was glad that her cousin was here to help!

She took the two boys to one side. "Contestants, your detective instincts are right. Something has gone wrong here. However, as you reached the final clue first, you are the winners."

The two boys didn't seem too pleased.

"But we wanted to find out who killed Poppy..."

"Don't worry, I'm not really dead. See?" Poppy did a little dance to prove how alive she was. This seemed to cheer them up a little.

"I'll tell the teachers to give you your prize, but I have one last mission for you." Zaiba put her hand on the little boy's shoulder. She needed to get them out of the room so that they could get on with the real investigation. "It's deadly serious. I need you to inform the rest of the competitors that the evidence has been tampered with, the trail is off for now."

"You can trust us!" The two boys flew out of the room, ready to perform their duty as trainee detectives.

"What next?" Mariam turned to Zaiba.

"What do you think the bin has to do with our case?" Poppy chipped in.

Two sets of eyes watched Zaiba, waiting to hear what she'd say next. "At the moment I only have one theory. Miss Grey is a science teacher, right?"

"Right!"

"She must have come in here to empty this bin, ignoring our DO NOT MOVE sign. But why?"

Poppy sucked her bottom lip. "Because she wanted to get rid of something?"

"Good thinking! Because she made the poison in here and needed to dispose of the evidence."

Mariam and Poppy were silent for a moment as they took this in and Zaiba patiently waited to see if they'd come on board with her theory. But as she opened her mouth to speak there was a commotion out in the hallway! People were shouting angrily. What about?

Zaiba ran to the door and pushed...

But it didn't budge.

"Come and help me!" she called to the others. Poppy and Mariam ran over, bracing their shoulders against the polished wood.

They tried again, all pushing together.

One ... two ... *three!*

The door still wouldn't move.

How could this be? Zaiba sank back against the door. "No, no, NO!" she cried. "Not now!"

"Is what I think is happening *actually* happening?" Poppy said in a faltering voice.

"I think it might be," Mariam added. Her bottom lip looked on the verge of a wobble.

Zaiba's hands fell to her sides in despair. "Things have taken a serious turn for the worse." She rattled the handle one last time in the hope that she could be wrong, but no luck. "We're locked in!"

12
SCIENCE LAB SOS

Locked in the science lab! This was *not* how Zaiba had planned to spend the rest of her day. They were finally closing in on the suspect and they'd been stopped in their tracks. But why? Who would do such a thing?

"I'm going to try and pick the lock with my hairpin," Poppy suggested, pulling a thin metal clip out of her hair.

"Have you ever done it before?" Mariam raised her eyebrows.

"*No*, but I've seen it in movies!" Poppy said. She started poking round in the keyhole but almost immediately the hair clip began to bend and collapse.

"I think it only works in the movies," Zaiba said gently.

"Good try though, Pops."

Grabbing a stool from the corner of the room, she climbed on it and peered out of the window at the top of the door.

She could finally see what the commotion was out in the corridor.

"It's Marco and Aunt Raim. They're shouting at each other!" Zaiba called down to the others.

"Uh-oh." A frown creased Mariam's brow. "She shouldn't be making herself look suspicious!"

Zaiba didn't point out to Mariam that Aunt Raim going on a shouty rampage in public was nothing out of the ordinary. But Marco ... Zaiba suddenly recalled how he had looked at her when she promised her dad that she'd solve the crime. Was he trying to stop her? Surely that raised him on the list of suspects, but she couldn't prove anything stuck in here!

Think, Zaiba. Think! What would Eden Lockett do? Aha!

"Pops, do you remember Eden Lockett's *The Case of the Shoplifter's Shoe?*"

"Of course! It's about clothes – it's obviously my

favourite one."

"When Eden gets locked in the changing room she calls for help by tapping SOS in Morse code on the door. She uses the heel of her shoe!"

They looked down at their shoes. Poppy was wearing her chunky boots, Mariam was wearing her jellies and Zaiba was wearing running shoes. Not a heel in sight.

Glancing round in desperation, Zaiba spotted a small, rubber hammer in one of the equipment trays. It would have to do!

"Right, who knows Morse code?" Zaiba said, secretly wishing she'd spent more time memorizing the cheat sheet included at the back of her Eden Lockett book.

"Ummmmmm..." Poppy pretended to be very interested in a mark on the table and Mariam looked just as blank.

"Can someone look it up then?" Zaiba sighed. A detective shouldn't really be relying on the internet but desperate times called for desperate measures!

Mariam wasn't allowed a mobile phone (another of Raim's rules) so Poppy got hers out and pulled up a page on Morse code.

"OK, it says SOS is dot, dot, dot, dash, dash, dash, dot, dot, dot."

Zaiba began tapping on the glass with the hammer, short and long taps.

Tap, tap, tap, tap … tap … tap … tap, tap, tap.

Then she realized the long taps didn't sound like long taps so she started dragging the hammer for those ones.

Tap, tap, tap, dragggg, dragggg, dragggg, tap, tap, tap.

But there was no movement from the other side of the door. Clearly no one could hear them over Aunt Raim's shouting!

"I don't think the hammer is loud enough," said Zaiba, whacking the door as hard as she could.

"You have to be more regular with the taps, it has to be the same rhythm." Poppy took the rubber hammer and tried doing it herself.

"It doesn't matter!" Mariam cut through them both. "No one will be able to hear over my mum and Marco shouting anyway."

The three of them slumped to the floor, backs against the locked door. Zaiba needed inspiration and she needed it fast. *Aunt Fouzia or Ammi would know what to do. They really understood detecting.*

Her hand grazed her yellow bag. Inspiration! Ammi had written little notes for Zaiba among the pages. Carefully she took out the Eden Lockett novel that she kept in there and flicked through it. She turned away slightly and opened up on the middle page. It was the part in the story where Eden had chased a suspect into an alley with a dead end. Zaiba traced an arrow from the sentence to the side of the page where her ammi had made a note: *If plan A doesn't work, there's a whole alphabet worth of letters left to try!*

Zaiba's eyes sparkled. Her ammi was right – they needed a plan B!

"OK, team!" She tucked away her book and turned to the girls. "It's time for plan B. Let's go back over the situation."

"Well, we're locked inside the science lab and we need to get through this door." Poppy knocked on the door behind her.

Something clicked in Zaiba's mind. "But is it actually locked? Let's check the latch!"

Level with the keyhole, Zaiba put her eye to the tiny gap between the side of the door and the doorframe.

"Light! I can see the light coming through. Of course – there's no bolt in place! The door isn't actually locked!" Zaiba grinned with exhilaration. "Why didn't I think of this before?" She got down on her hands and knees and looked underneath the door. She moved from the left-hand side closest to the hinge and steadily across until she came to a spot where the light was blocked.

"Here!" She gestured to the others. "There's something wedged underneath the door, blocking it from opening!"

Poppy dropped to her knees and peered under too. "It looks like some folded-up paper," she mumbled, her face still half pressed to the ground.

"All we have to do is push it out and the door will open. Everyone, look for something that's strong enough to unblock it!"

The trio scrambled to their feet and began searching around the room. Mariam held up the metal gauze that goes over a Bunsen burner but shook her head – not long enough. Poppy found an exercise book but it was too thick to go under the door. Finally Zaiba opened up a drawer underneath the worktop and found a metal ruler; thin, strong and long – perfect!

Rushing back to the door, Zaiba got down and lay on her tummy. Then she wriggled the ruler underneath the door and began jabbing at the paper.

"It's really jammed in!" she grunted between pokes.

"Keep going!" Poppy urged.

A chunk of paper tore off leaving the rest of the wedge small enough for Zaiba to prod hard and – *POP!* The door was unjammed.

"Thank goodness!" Mariam cried, throwing the door open. "I thought we'd be stuck in there forever."

Poppy bent down and picked up the wedge of paper. As she unfurled it, Mariam and Zaiba came to look over her shoulder.

It was some torn-out pages from a copy of *Unicats*.

"Who could vandalize a book like that?" Poppy gasped.

"And more importantly, who would have a spare copy of *Unicats* to hand?" Zaiba said in a low voice.

All three girls slowly gazed up to where Marco was standing at the end of the corridor, red-faced and still shouting at Raim. What had Poppy mentioned earlier? That he was married to the author of *Unicats*? He'd have access to loads of those books.

"More like Uni*rat*..." Poppy shook her head.

Things certainly didn't look good for Marco Romano.

13
NEW EVIDENCE

Out in the school's main hallway, Marco and Raim were having the argument of the century. It was like watching a lion and a shark going head to head.

"It's so awful, but I can't look away," Poppy said, her eyes wide.

Zaiba managed to pick out the odd snatch of words:

"YOU DON'T DESERVE TO WIN!"

"YOUR BAKING TASTES LIKE OLD SOCKS!"

"I BET YOU USED INSTANT CAKE MIX!"

"We have to stop this!" Mariam rushed over to her mum and pulled on her arm, trying to drag her away. Poppy started to hurry over to help but Zaiba held her back.

"Don't get involved," she whispered. "Not when they're this angry."

Thomas Hanlon had joined them and was trying to break the pair up.

"Come on!" he yelled, restraining Marco. "There are children present!"

In one swoop Marco *pushed* Thomas off him causing the school governor to topple over to the floor with a hard thud. A silence fell over the corridor. Out of nowhere the deputy head rushed forwards and dropped to her knees by his side.

"Oh, darling, are you OK?" Miss Grey gushed, stroking his face.

"Ewwww," Poppy screwed up her face. "More old people in love!"

"So gross." Ali sidled up beside them. The commotion was so loud it had even been heard in the school hall and he'd come out to investigate like a true detective.

Zaiba watched as Miss Grey's eyes widened. She'd given away their secret romance!

Is the poisoning another case of two criminals working
together, Zaiba thought. *Like the sneaky Stevens siblings in*
the case of the missing diamond collar? Maybe the deputy head
and Thomas Hanlon are in on it together.

At the end of the central corridor, hiding behind some
lockers, Zaiba spotted a head of black curls, then two big
eyes peeping out at the scene. Gabriele! He saw Zaiba
and finally emerged, running up to her with tearful
eyes. Zaiba and Poppy gave him a reassuring hug and Ali
patted him on the back.

"It's OK, Gabs," Poppy soothed him. "Thomas isn't
hurt."

"Why don't you tell us what you found in the school
hall?" Zaiba prompted.

Gabriele wiped his eyes and looked up, sniffing. "The
compere was hired from an agency. He's never been here
before so he has no motive to poison the cakes."

"Great info, Gabriele," Zaiba encouraged. "Ali, any
updates?"

"You bet!" Ali replied. "Sam got the results back from
the lab. The poison in Ms Goremain's bloodstream is

called grayanotoxin. I haven't had time to research it yet though!"

Zaiba's eyes narrowed. So they had the name of the toxin ... but that didn't tell them anything about who had poisoned the cake. She looked over at Marco, who was huffing and puffing, his cheeks turning red. Gabriele was looking too, his almond eyes wide with worry.

"It's so embarrassing! Why do parents have to be so over the top in competitions?" he said, wringing his hands.

"I know, right? It's supposed to be fun!" Ali shook his head. "Did you know that competitive people are more likely to have high blood pressure?"

Zaiba shushed him. Now wasn't the best time for one of his interesting facts.

"My dad is *so* competitive." Gabriele was getting fired up. "He even put a rose petal on the cake for the Lady Mayor because he knows she loves roses. That's basically bribery!"

Zaiba paused. "Wait, the rose-petal cake was meant for the Lady Mayor?"

Gabriele nodded but before he could say more, his dad called over to him.

"Gabriele, come. Let's get some fresh air." Marco shot one last hard look at Raim, who was sitting quietly with Mariam on a bench, and stormed out to the playground.

Raim's arm gripped tighter round Mariam's shoulders – she clearly wasn't going to let her daughter out of her sight. Mariam mouthed, "Sorry!" at Zaiba and shrugged. Gabriele huffed and reluctantly followed his dad, but not before Ali gave him one last encouraging hug. Zaiba was proud of her brother – a good secret agent should show empathy.

"Ali, did you get your camera back from the receptionist?" Zaiba pressed as soon as Gabriele was out of earshot.

"Yes... Why do you want to know?" She could hear the caution in her brother's voice. After all, the last time he'd handed his camera to Zaiba she'd chucked it under a storage unit door!

"I need to see the photos you took of the tasting again. I think we missed something."

Ali pulled out his camera and flicked through the photos to the moment of the tasting.

"There!" Zaiba pointed to an image of the head teacher, holding a cupcake to her mouth. "Ms Goremain is eating the cupcake with the rose petal on – the one that was supposed to go to the Lady Mayor."

"I remember now!" Poppy gasped. "That's why I thought Ms Goremain was holding a flower – because of the petal. When she was clutching her throat, a rose petal fell off the cake."

Zaiba's head started spinning with all the clues and evidence they'd picked up together. "If the rose-petal cake was *specifically* meant to go to the Lady Mayor but it got swapped *and* it was the last cupcake Ms Goremain tasted before she had the reaction..." She stared at the others. "Doesn't that mean it has the highest chance of being the poisoned cupcake?"

"Yes, I guess it does." Ali frowned, trying to keep up with Zaiba's theory.

She was still thinking hard, piecing together the information. "What if Ms Goremain wasn't supposed to be poisoned? What if—"

"The poison went to the wrong victim!" Poppy exclaimed, snapping her fingers.

Zaiba gave Ali his camera back and reached into her bag. She opened up *The Flower Show Felony*. She searched through the pages in a rush before coming to the right page. "Here, look at this!"

Poppy leaned over, breathing fast, and read out another of Ammi's notes: *Don't just question what HAS happened, question what HASN'T happened. You have to question EVERYTHING.*

Ali, Zaiba and Poppy looked at each other, stunned.

Zaiba flipped open her notebook. "This changes everything!"

Gazing at her list of suspects she revisited each one, then clicked her phone recorder on.

"New evidence has come to light. If the Lady Mayor was the intended victim that definitely rules out Peter the caretaker, since he likes her. The deputy head and Thomas Hanlon have no obvious motive to poison her, neither do Aunt Raim and Dad." She crossed the names out as she went. "That leaves one person..."

Together they looked down at the only name that hadn't been crossed out: *Marco*.

Ali grabbed the phone from Zaiba and spoke into it: "The Lady Mayor was meant to eat a specific cake but she didn't – Ms Goremain ate it instead. It seems probable that this was the poisoned cake and the Lady Mayor was the intended victim."

Zaiba high-fived Ali – his logical brain was vital in their investigations.

"*And* it was one of Marco's cakes – which he wouldn't let Gabriele try! I remember thinking that was strange! His cakes were going to be tested by the Lady Mayor, who has judged this competition for the last thirty years!" Poppy added into the recorder.

"So she would have been judging the baking competition when Marco was at school. She was the one to always give him second place!" Zaiba concluded, clicking off the phone recorder.

Together as a team they had pieced together the suspect, the motive and the opportunity! Marco wanted revenge on the woman who had always stopped him from coming first, and this baking competition had been his chance.

"There's one last thing to figure out. How did the cakes get swapped?" Ali asked.

Zaiba packed up her notebook, pens and Eden Lockett book. "I think I know who to ask, and she's wearing a green dress with red roses."

14
BEAUTIFUL BUT DEADLY

"If I were the Lady Mayor, where would I be?" Zaiba tapped her temple. That woman loved attention. She smiled. "Centre stage!"

Zaiba, Poppy and Ali flew back out on to the village green, where they found the Lady Mayor STILL standing on the little stage erected for the jazz trio, who were playing a medley of dance tunes. One or two couples moved around the common in what Zaiba guessed was a waltz. But the Lady Mayor was ignoring them from her place up on the stage. She was busy addressing her adoring crowd – made up of two parents, three teachers and a dog.

"Bean!" Poppy ran up to her pooch, who was sitting patiently at her mum's feet.

"I've been waiting here for a good twenty minutes to find out whether the dog show judging is going ahead," Poppy's mum huffed. "The Lady Mayor is supposed to be compering, but all she's doing at the moment is blabbing to anyone who will listen."

Zaiba and Poppy watched as the Lady Mayor walked over to the band's singer and prised the microphone from his hands.

"Excuse me, I'm so sorry for interrupting the proceedings but I thought I should make a statement at this dreadful time," she bellowed far too loudly into the microphone and there was a high-pitched wail that had everyone throwing their hands to their ears.

Zaiba, Poppy and Ali collectively rolled their eyes.

The Lady Mayor tapped the microphone as though the screech had been a technical issue, not down to her bellowing. "As I was saying..." She gave a wide smile to the gathered crowd and moved her hand in what looked like a royal wave.

"Why is she shouting? They could probably hear her in the North Pole!" Ali winced, covering his ears.

"She wants the people over in the school to hear." Zaiba imagined her dad and stepmum still huddled in the hall, waiting for some news about what had happened to Ms Goremain.

The Lady Mayor went on. "Though the health of our head teacher steadily improves, let us not forget the pain that she, *and I*, have endured." She bit her lip as though calling on extra supplies of inner strength. "The summer fete should be a time of celebration and merriment in our village. Therefore, despite this *great tragedy* we must continue with brave hearts and heads held high. It's what Ms Goremain would want. Thank you."

There was an awkward silence, which one lone audience member filled with a few sad claps. Thankfully the band started up again as the Lady Mayor finally handed back the microphone.

"Can you imagine what she'd have been like if she *had* been poisoned? Although at least she wouldn't be able to talk," Ali whispered. Zaiba swiftly whacked him on the arm but not without a smirk.

Now was their chance to question the Lady Mayor.

They rushed up to her as she descended the little set of wooden stairs to the side of the stage.

"Excuse me, Your Highness!" Poppy declared, holding out her hands.

"We mean, Lady Mayor," Zaiba corrected her. "Would you have a moment to talk about your terrible experience at the tasting. You've been so brave."

The Lady Mayor's eyes lit up. "I suppose I could spare a few minutes. It has been such a long day."

"The average adult woman is awake for sixteen hours a day and it's only twenty to four. So you still have at least seven more hours left of your day." Ali peered up at her with big eyes.

"What a clever boy!" The Lady Mayor seemed impressed.

Zaiba needed to get the conversation back on track. "We wanted to ask you about the moment of the tasting. Were there any cakes in particular that caught your eye?"

The Lady Mayor paused for a moment, her lips pursed. "Why, yes. On the last batch of cakes there was a cupcake topped with a beautiful rose petal. Roses are, of course, my favourite flower and the cake was on my plate for the tasting."

"And was that the cake you tasted?" Zaiba pressed.

"Actually, no. Just before we put on our blindfolds, Ms Goremain commented on how pretty my cake was, so as a gesture of goodwill I swapped with her." She gave a small, proud smile. "I always like to give an extra warm welcome to any new teachers. I wanted her to feel special."

"Brilliant, thank you!" Zaiba had the confirmation she'd needed. Now there was no time to lose. She needed to inform the head teacher on this latest development – to explain that what happened was all a terrible mistake. Starting at the school must have been a terrible strain for Ms Goremain. Zaiba could imagine how it felt to be new. But now she could reassure the head teacher that no one hated her. And Zaiba doubted the Lady Mayor would be too upset by the news – she would probably love all the attention!

Grabbing Ali's hand, and with one last smile, she rushed away but Poppy lingered a moment. "Also, could you go and judge my mum's dog show please? She's worked really hard on it. Thank you!"

Zaiba glanced back and saw her bob a curtsy then run after them towards the school, leaving the Lady Mayor smiling after her.

Ms Goremain was still recuperating in her office when Zaiba, Poppy and Ali knocked rapidly on the door. To their surprise, the deputy head answered.

"Can I help you?" Miss Grey glared down at the three of them.

"I have some important news for Ms Goremain regarding the poisoning," Zaiba said in her most official tone. "We're here representing the Snow Leopard Detective Agency UK."

The deputy head scowled and began to protest. "I'm really not sure—"

But Ms Goremain called from inside the office, "Let them in!"

Sam was back in the office, having taken the blood test away for results. She was keeping a close eye on the head teacher who was sitting at her desk with her legs propped up on another chair. A huge pitcher of water was placed in front of her and Zaiba noticed that she'd already drunk three quarters of it. The fluids must have been working because Ms Goremain was looking much better. The pink had returned to her cheeks and her voice sounded less strained. Sam really was a brilliant doctor!

"What news do you have for me, Miss Shah?" Ms Goremain gestured Zaiba to sit down in the chair opposite her desk, Poppy and Ali flanking her.

"From our investigations, we believe that the poisoned cupcake must have been in the final batch for tasting. And we have deduced that it was the cupcake with the rose petal on top."

"That fits with the results from the hospital," Sam added. "They said that the poison was fast-acting."

"Yes, it was after eating the last cupcake that I started coughing." Ms Goremain seemed unimpressed so far.

"But that cupcake wasn't given to you for tasting. It was originally meant for the Lady Mayor," Poppy explained.

Ms Goremain's eyes widened and she suddenly sat up straight. "I'd totally forgotten that we swapped! But that would imply..."

"Exactly." Zaiba nodded. "You weren't the intended victim. It was the Lady Mayor who was supposed to be poisoned."

The new head teacher exhaled deeply and leaned back in her chair. "To be honest, I'm relieved." She looked over at the deputy head. "I hope you won't mind me saying, but I was a bit worried that you were out to get me."

Miss Grey blushed and looked at her feet. "Celia, I know I haven't behaved as best I could, but I never would have poisoned you! It was just difficult for me to accept a new person on the team." She swallowed hard. The next words clearly cost her a lot. "But I apologize."

Ms Goremain waved a hand through the air, immediately making the mood much lighter. "No, no. I think we both could have behaved better. I was so eager to start here, I didn't really stop to think about how other people would feel. But I really would like to listen to your ideas for the school and for us to be more of a team. Starting with you getting a bigger office!"

"That would be nice!" The deputy head smiled. "And I must apologize for Thomas being in your office earlier. We've had to have meetings in here as my office isn't big enough."

Zaiba raised her eyebrows. She wasn't sure that secret romantic conversations counted as meetings but she was glad that the two heads of the school had come to an understanding.

"I'd like to point out that even though we've got the real victim and the poison identified, we still don't know who did it!" Zaiba said, trying to get the teachers to understand the severity of the situation.

What she didn't mention was that they had a prime suspect – who had both motive and opportunity. But they needed to prove that Marco had poisoned the cake before making any allegations. And where had he got the poison? They still hadn't managed to dig to the bottom of *that* mystery either.

"Perhaps we can get a greater budget for the science lab equipment..." Ms Goremain had stopped listening to Zaiba and was still discussing plans with the deputy head, who had pulled up a chair to start making notes. Sam and the team of detectives could have been flying around the room and the women wouldn't have noticed they were so deep in conversation.

But listening to their discussion had unlocked a door in Zaiba's brain. An image flashed up in her mind. The science lab. She thought back to the bin there – the one that should have contained evidence for her detective trail. Could that contain the answer? Maybe they would find the final piece of the puzzle there.

"Ali." She turned to her younger brother. "I need you to research that poison."

Zaiba had a theory, and there was only one way to prove it.

"Detective rule number fifteen!" Zaiba cried, throwing open the door to the science lab. *"The smallest detail could be the biggest clue!"*

Poppy and Ali, still clicking away on his phone, bounded through the door and joined Zaiba, who was staring intently inside the bin.

"Careful not to get locked in this time," came a voice from the door. It was Mariam, propping the door open with a chair. "I snuck away from my mum the moment she calmed down." Her eyes glittered with excitement. "I guess you've got me hooked on investigating."

Zaiba beamed and beckoned her over. "It's all about the petals. They're the key to this case. Petals like these."

She started to reach down into the bin but Ali pulled her hand back.

"Mad honey disease!" he yelled.

"Excuse me?" Zaiba raised an eyebrow.

Ali flipped his phone screen round to show Zaiba what he was looking at. "Grayanotoxin poisoning –

also known as mad honey disease. It comes from the Ericaceae family of plants. Specifically in the honey and the nectar. Side effects can be confusion, nausea, low heart rate ... sometimes even death."

Zaiba couldn't breathe. "What types of plant are in that family?"

Ali looked at the list on his phone and started reeling them off. "Erica, cassiope, rhododendron, calluna—"

"Wait!" Zaiba looked down into the bin. Those bright pink petals... She'd seen them earlier in the public gardens.

"These are rhododendron petals!" Zaiba felt like jumping up and down.

"A rhodo-what?" Poppy looked to Zaiba and then Ali for answers.

"It's a type of flower and there are some rhododendron plants on the village green." Zaiba thought back to that morning's walk through the gardens and the flowers that had been torn up. "So that's where those missing flower heads went."

All four of them gazed down at the torn-up petals

in the bin. This was where the poison had come from. Clearly the evidence had then been hastily discarded in the bin. Too hastily!

"Everyone split up and search the room. There must be some evidence of Marco in here. And be careful, don't touch anything suspicious."

Poppy, Ali and Mariam began searching the room as Zaiba carefully lifted the bin up on to a stool where she could see inside more easily. To think something as pretty as a flower petal could be poisonous!

"Here!" Mariam called from inside a cupboard. Using a cloth over her hand like a glove she carefully carried out a small pot. "Look. This was underneath a cabinet with textbooks in – someone must have hidden it there."

"Well done, Mariam." Zaiba took the pot from her and placed it on the desk, inspecting the contents. It seemed to be a dark red sticky goo.

"That looks exactly like mad honey," Ali confirmed with a nod. "The nectar or honey from rhododendrons is the most poisonous. You really wouldn't want to spread that on your toast!"

"Um, Zaiba, I've got something else here," Poppy mumbled from underneath the teacher's desk. She emerged holding a spatula with the hem of her dress. Poppy knew the importance of preserving the fingerprints on evidence – it was in all of Eden Lockett's novels.

"I don't think they even need fingerprints for this one." Poppy dropped the spatula down on the desk next to the pot of honey. "It has his initials on it."

Looking closely at the handle of the spatula, Zaiba noticed the letters M.R. in gold lettering. "Marco Romano... He must have hidden the evidence here to come and collect later."

"As if the posioned cake wasn't enough!" Mariam shook her head. "He used poisonous glaze too!"

Zaiba had to agree with her cousin – this was low, even for Marco. "The police will have to get the glaze tested, to confirm the poison matches that in Ms Goremain's bloodstream. But I think we've got him."

There was a sudden squeak of speakers and an announcement was made over the school tannoy system.

"This is Celia Goremain, head teacher speaking. I'd like to thank everyone for their concern but I can assure you I am now fine. A little weak but nonetheless I will be returning to the fete. Our school will not be shaken by this event and the fete will *not* be cancelled. I will be meeting with the baking contestants in the school hall for a private meeting before joining everyone back on the village green. Everyone else, carry on and enjoy the sunshine."

There was a momentary pause before Ms Goremain spoke again. "One more thing. Would the Snow Leopard Detective Agency – UK branch – please report to the school hall. Immediately."

15
A KILLER COMPETITIVE STREAK

In the school hall, the tension was as high as the *Great British Bake Off* final on Channel Four. Marco, Raim and Hassan had been put in different corners of the room to avoid any more altercations.

The summer heat was getting to them all. Raim was gently perspiring and Marco had huge sweat patches sticking his pink shirt to his back.

As Zaiba walked further into the hall she realized that the head teacher didn't want a meeting, she wanted answers.

"Good, you're here." Ms Goremain smiled as the children approached. "Peter, can you stay by the door to make sure we aren't disturbed?"

The caretaker obliged, positioning himself by the double doors and slamming them shut. There was no breeze at all and the air around them was still and silent. Ms Goremain had managed to gather Peter, the baking contestants, the deputy head, Thomas Hanlon and finally the Lady Mayor, who had changed into a white flowing sundress and floppy hat. When she'd found the time to change, Zaiba had no idea.

Ms Goremain turned to Zaiba. "When you mentioned the Snow Leopard Detective Agency, I knew I could trust your investigation. Your aunt Fouzia rang me after Samirah told her what had happened. She's a brilliant woman, as is her daughter."

Zaiba flushed with pride, her chest filling with love for her aunt who lived so far away and her clever, confident cousin.

Thomas Hanlon stepped forwards. "Celia, are you sure you can trust a student to conduct an investigation—"

"I trust the children of our school completely."

She paused and gazed at Zaiba. "This young detective is an especially bright student. I would like to hear her findings. Our children's voices are as important as our own."

Zaiba felt the blood rush to her cheeks. Their new head teacher had called her a young detective!

Thomas Hanlon immediately stepped back and Zaiba saw the fiery look of determination in Ms Goremain's eyes. No wonder she had been made head teacher – everyone in the room could see how much she cared about the school and its children!

Poppy grabbed Zaiba's hand and squeezed it tight. "You've got this, Zai," she whispered and Ali nodded in agreement. Even Mariam gave her a thumbs up from behind the little trolley they'd wheeled in, holding the evidence. Taking a deep breath, Zaiba climbed up on to one of the school benches. Aunt Fouzia had once told her that making yourself seem bigger was an effective way to feel confident when addressing a group. Not to mention it meant she could see everyone in the room and they could see her. It was time to reveal her findings.

"Firstly, it's important that everyone knows that we conducted this investigation fairly. I considered each suspect equally, including my own dad." She looked over at Hassan, who was gazing back at her proudly. It took a lot for him to support her detective ambitions, especially after what happened to her ammi. Zaiba smiled at him and he winked back.

"But after one key finding, everything fell into place. Lady Mayor, would you mind telling everyone which cake you were given to taste in the last batch?"

"The cake with the rose petal on top." The Lady Mayor spoke from a reclining chair that had been especially brought in for her.

"Ms Goremain, which cake were you given to taste?"

"I was given the cupcake with the violet on top," Ms Goremain addressed the room.

Right on cue, Ali pulled up the picture of the tasting on his camera and began walking round the room, showing each person the photo from the tasting.

"But those were not the cakes they ate. You see, the

Lady Mayor kindly swapped her cake with Ms Goremain at the last minute, after the head teacher had admired it. It was after eating that cake that Ms Goremain had the reaction. This proves it. The rose-petal cupcake was the poisoned cake."

"That wasn't my batch!" Raim called out.

"No, it wasn't," Zaiba agreed. "It wasn't my dad's either."

Everyone in the room turned to look at Marco, whose shirt was now almost see-through with sweat.

A little voice piped up from behind Marco – it was Gabriele and he was furious.

"So that's why you wouldn't let me try the cake, Dad! It was poisoned!"

Marco hastily shushed his son. "That doesn't mean it was me. Someone must have tampered with my cakes!" He ran his sweaty hands through his hair. Zaiba watched them tremble.

"Just before the baking began, Mr Romano," she said, "you bumped into me as you rushed out of the tent towards the school. What were you doing?"

Marco stuttered and spluttered before he managed to say, "Melting my butter for – for my glaze."

"A glaze you had to make in secret because it contained *poison*. A glaze like *this*?" Zaiba gestured to Mariam, who wheeled forward a tray holding the pot of honey, the spatula and the bin.

"Exhibit A is a pot of rhododendron nectar – mad honey – found in the science lab. Alongside exhibit B, a bin containing rhododendron petals, and exhibit C, a spatula engraved with Marco's initials, all found in the science lab. Rhododendrons contain a toxin called grayanotoxin, the same poison found in Ms Goremain's blood test."

"A few petals in a bin don't prove anything! That spatula must have been planted there by the real criminal."

"I didn't want to bring this up, Mr Romano." Zaiba remained calm. "But while my team were investigating in the science lab earlier, we were locked in by a jammed door. It had been jammed using these pages of *Unicats*." Zaiba pulled out the wedge of paper from her pocket and held them up to the room.

"You locked my daughter in the science lab?" Hassan roared, but Zaiba gestured for him to keep his cool.

"Marco Romano," Zaiba rounded up, going in for the kill. "I believe that you tried to poison the Lady Mayor because after years of coming second place in the baking competitions she judged, you are competitive and bitter. I believe you used the rhododendron flowers from the public gardens – there are flower heads missing – to poison the cake. Then when your plan went wrong and Ms Goremain was poisoned instead, you became angry. You've been running about the school ranting ever since. You tried to stop our investigation when you saw us in the science lab, where you had hidden your evidence, planning to dispose of it later. And in the process you threw away the last clue in my detective trail – disappointing many budding detectives, by the way! Samirah has the results of the poisoning outside in the first-aid tent."

Zaiba exhaled and looked Marco square in the eye.

He was shaking, bright red and sweating profusely ... but keeping very quiet. Ms Goremain's face was flushed with pride as she watched and Zaiba noticed that her dad's eyes were brimming. *Are those tears?* Jessica had placed a comforting hand on his shoulder and she gave Zaiba a slow nod of approval. Zaiba was only sad that Aunt Fouzia couldn't be here to witness this moment.

"I have a poison-detector kit in the science lab, Marco," the deputy head spoke up. "I could go and check that honey in a matter of minutes..."

Suddenly Marco let out a wail that filled the hall.

"OK! OK! Fine." He put his head in his hands. "It was me."

The Lady Mayor gasped and clutched her heart. Peter rushed forwards and gave her a glass of water from the canteen counter.

"Oh, for goodness' sake!" Marco strode up and down the hall. "Thirty years! Thirty years that woman has never once put me in first place! I thought that if I could get her off the judging panel *just this once* I might actually win. I deserve to win!"

"So you poisoned her?" Ms Goremain looked disgusted.

"I put a *little* bit of rhododendron in the cake," Marco cried. "But then when I got here, I remembered how *unfair* it all is. And that's when I added the honey, so she would really learn a lesson!"

Everyone was staring at Marco. Raim was open-mouthed, Hassan looked like he was ready to tackle him, and everyone else was shaking their heads in dismay. As Marco looked from face to face, his expression suddenly broke from anger to stark realization.

"Oh no," he said quietly. "What have I done?" He sat down heavily.

Ms Goremain walked up to Marco and took Gabriele's hand to come and stand with her. "Marco, it goes without saying that you are henceforth banned from all future baking competitions. And where are the police? Thomas, I thought you rang them?"

Thomas Hanlon gritted his teeth awkwardly, "Oh, I uh... Actually, I didn't call the police." He turned to Miss

Grey. "I wasn't sure if you were involved, so I went to see if there was any evidence I could dispose of, starting in Celia's office, in case you had left something after one of our meetings. Then I forgot to call the police in all the chaos that followed."

Miss Grey looked a little shocked. "You thought I was a suspect?"

Mr Hanlon's face paled and he began to talk quickly. "Only in the most academic sense. But then I remembered how good your heart is and—"

She threw her arms around him before he could finish explaining. "Oh, darling, you tried to protect me!"

Zaiba noticed Poppy sticking her tongue out again and she had to agree, *gross*.

"So who is going to call the police?" Zaiba announced, slightly annoyed that she'd been solving this crime against a false deadline.

There was a moment of silence before, **WHAM**!

"I'M HERE, NOBODY PANIC!"

A man in a police uniform burst through the double doors of the school hall, puffing and panting, his cheeks red. It was the police chief!

The whole hall collectively groaned.

"Right, what do we have here?" the chief bellowed, hitching up his belt and pacing about the hall. "I received a call from a concerned parent. Something about poison? A poisonous gas no doubt through the air vents, it does smell a bit whiffy in here!"

He got out a little flip pad and started scribbling down what Zaiba guessed was a load of old nonsense.

"Actually, Chief." The Lady Mayor slowly rose from her chair. "The crime has already been solved."

The chief's eyes bugged. "Lady Mayor, I didn't see you there. Wh-what do you mean it's been solved?"

"This young detective and her agency have solved the whole case." The Lady Mayor gestured to Zaiba and the police chief looked as though his eyes might pop out of his head.

"But she's just a child!" The chief started laughing haughtily but quickly stopped when he realized that the other people in the hall were not joining in.

"I'm sure she'll run it all by you later, if you ask her

nicely. And then you can issue Mr Romano here with a warning. But for now, I have something to say." The Lady Mayor, assisted by Peter, took her place in the centre of the room. She ushered Ms Goremain and the police chief to go and sit down. "I have known Marco since he was a small boy." Marco looked up from where he was sitting and Zaiba could see his face was full of regret. "He has always been desperate to impress. He puts himself under an immense amount of pressure. So much so that he drove himself to commit a terrible act today!"

The Lady Mayor approached Marco. "You may be a very silly man, Marco Romano, but you are no criminal. The police will issue you with a warning and keep a close eye on you. But I believe that you are capable of losing this ridiculous competitive streak. I would like you to channel all that energy into helping me with projects in the local community. What do we always tell the children? Coming first is not the most important thing!"

Marco nodded his head slowly, and though he looked

like he'd rather go to prison than spend time with the Lady Mayor, he seemed relieved.

"I'm sorry," he said in a quiet voice. "Especially to you, Gabriele. This should have been a fun thing for us to do together and I ruined it."

Gabriele let go of Ms Goremain's hand and went over to his dad. "It's OK, Dad. Thank you for apologizing."

Zaiba felt her shoulders relax and she got down from the bench to join her team.

"And, of course, this reminds me of a story about the importance of good sportsmanship..." The Lady Mayor launched into a speech. In the closed-off school hall she had a captive audience!

"What have we done to deserve this?" Ali whispered. "Now we have to listen to a whole lecture on the difference between right and wrong."

"Which we already know!" Poppy whispered back.

"We know more than that." Mariam leaned in. "Enough to solve a poisoning all on our own."

"It was good to have you as part of the team." Zaiba smiled at her cousin. Maybe they could be friends after all.

"You're absolutely right, Lady Mayor." Ms Goremain clapped her hands, saving everyone from listening to another half an hour of speech. "But we must get back to the fete-goers outside. It's not the end of the day yet!"

"What about my investigation?" the police chief protested, his hands on his hips.

"I'd be happy to give you a full statement," Zaiba stepped forwards, holding out her hand for him to shake. "Agent Zaiba of the Snow Leopard Detective Agency UK."

The police chief paused for a moment but then shook it. "Well, all right then. Where did you say you worked again?"

As Zaiba filled in the police chief, everyone in the room stirred, stretching their arms and getting to their feet. The case had been solved and justice, in its own way, was served. Spending that much time with the Lady Mayor was punishment enough. It was time to enjoy the rest of the day and, most of all, get out of the stuffy hall.

Ms Goremain turned to Raim, Mariam, Hassan and Ali, a glint in her eye. "Right everyone, we have some cakes to taste. The baking competition is back on!"

16
AND THE WINNER IS...

"I got these from the supermarket, so I know they are definitely poison-free!" The receptionist placed a family-sized pack of plain fairy cakes on to the countertop.

It seemed like every single person at the fete was crammed into the baking tent, eager to see who would finally be crowned winner. As Marco had been banned, it was down to two teams in a head-to-head battle. Raim with Mariam, and Hassan with Ali.

The teams would be judged solely on their decoration of the store-bought cakes.

Zaiba gripped Poppy and her mum's hands tightly as they watched the teams work. They bustled away over the shiny metal countertops, whipping, icing and piping two completely new designs. Zaiba noticed her dad carefully slicing open a vanilla bean pod and Ali scraping the contents into a bowl of buttercream. Delicious!

"Do you think they'll win?" Zaiba asked Jessica, not daring to peel her eyes away from the contest.

"I certainly hope so." Jessica puffed out her cheeks. "Or your dad is going to be very grumpy for the foreseeable future!"

An egg timer ticked down the last few seconds and the crowd began to chant.

"Ten, nine, eight, seven ..."

Hassan doused a sprinkle of gold dust over their cakes.

"Six, five, four ..."

Raim stuck a tiny flag in the centre of each cake.

"Three, TWO, ONE!"

"Bakers, step away from your cakes," the Lady Mayor announced, approaching the workstations.

The crowd fell silent as they watched the Lady

Mayor, now a lone judge and not blindfolded this time, surveying the cupcakes. She popped on a pair of impossibly thin reading glasses with pointed wings and started to inspect Raim and Mariam's cakes first. Zaiba noticed Mariam and her mum holding hands as they watched the Lady Mayor take a bite.

Keeping an entirely straight face, the Lady Mayor swallowed, paused and didn't say a word.

She then walked over silently to Hassan and Ali's counter. Zaiba's heart beat a little faster.

After what felt like an eternity of chewing, the Lady Mayor finally turned back to the audience and lowered her glasses. "I have made my decision."

The crowd leaned forwards in their seats and someone began doing a drumroll on a tabletop.

"The winning team of this year's parent-child baking competition for ingenious flavour complexity and a stunning design is ... Hassan and Ali!"

The crowd erupted into cheers and Zaiba couldn't help springing to her feet, clapping.

Hassan shook hands with Raim, who seemed to be

taking the loss surprisingly well, and then lifted Ali into the air in triumph.

"Dad, put me down! I think Mr Thompson is finally in the Soak the Teacher stocks!" Ali cried, peering out of the gap in the plastic windows.

Everyone laughed and Hassan lowered Ali back down so that he could run out of the tent – before he'd had a chance to accept their trophy from the Lady Mayor!

"And don't forget your prize. A free baking class at Madame Butterpuff's Patisserie!"

The Lady Mayor handed a gold envelope to Hassan and he looked like he might burst with excitement. The two of them posed for a quick photo before Hassan ventured into the crowd to find his family.

"Well done, Dad! I knew you could do it." Zaiba put her arms round his tummy and gave him a big squeeze.

"And I knew *you* could solve the crime." Hassan tapped her on the nose.

"Congratulations," Poppy sang happily. "The best team did win!"

"They did indeed," Jessica agreed, giving Hassan a kiss on the cheek.

Hassan wiped his forehead with a handkerchief. "All right, enough about me. Let's go out in the breeze and see how your brother's getting on at Soak the Teacher!"

Zaiba and Poppy rushed ahead and quickly spotted Ali lining up his shot. Mr Thompson was in the stocks sticking his tongue out before Ali hurled the missile. The sopping-wet sponge flew through the air with surprisingly good aim and got the teacher right in the face!

Snap! A photographer took a photo right at the moment of impact and smiled. "This will be perfect for the front cover."

Mr Thompson grimaced. "Yeah, *perfect*."

Zaiba saw Raim and Mariam approaching them from the baking tent. Mariam had her backpack on and Raim was holding a Tupperware box filled with cupcakes.

"We're going home now, Zaiba," said Mariam sadly.

"But I was going to suggest something fun!" Zaiba

looked up at her aunt. "Could we have another ten minutes, Aunt Raim, please?"

Aunt Raim tapped her foot on the ground but relented. "OK. But ten minutes *only!*"

"*Yes!* Come on." Zaiba grabbed Mariam's and Poppy's hands and rushed them over to the face-painting stand where Jessica was finally free of a queue.

"Do you know what you want, girls?" Jessica asked, picking up a sponge.

"Oh yeah!" Zaiba grinned.

Seven minutes later – and with the help of another face-painting artist – Mariam, Zaiba and Poppy emerged from the stand as new people. Well, maybe not *people*.

Zaiba was a snow leopard, complete with a spotted pattern and whiskers. Poppy was a butterfly (in colours matching her blue outfit of course) and Mariam ... Mariam was a pufferfish.

"Why did you choose that?' Poppy asked her, not understanding why anyone would want to be anything *but* a beautiful butterfly.

"So that I can do this!" Mariam blew out her cheeks

and it looked like her pufferfish had inflated. Zaiba and Poppy burst into laughter – maybe Mariam could hang out with them a bit more in the future.

"Do that again!" Jessica pulled out her phone and motioned to the girls to take up position.

Zaiba and Poppy threw their arms round Mariam as she puffed out her face again.

"Ready when you are!" Poppy cried, putting on her best pose. Jessica bit her lip as she took the photos, as though trying not to laugh. Then she showed them the phone screen. The three of them made the perfect trio, apart from one tiny detail. From behind the girls were two sets of familiar fingers making rabbit ears above Poppy and Zaiba's heads.

"We've been photobombed!" Poppy cried.

Zaiba swivelled round to grab her brother. "That's not funny!" she said, but she couldn't help laughing. It was a *bit* funny.

Ali wriggled away. "You need to work on your detective hearing," he teased.

Aunt Raim came over to the face-painting stand to

collect Mariam. At the sight of her daughter's happy face, she smiled. "Come on, my little pufferfish," she said, more softly than she'd spoken all day. "Time to go."

"See you later, Zaiba. Bye, Poppy," Mariam said shyly.

"And what did you want to say?" Raim prompted.

"I wanted to say thank you for letting me be part of the investigation. I had a really good day." Mariam smiled.

"We loved having you in the team." Zaiba grinned back.

"I'm very impressed by you all," Raim said. "I never knew Mariam had such good detective instincts. We'll see you again soon."

Then with a quick wave to Hassan and Jessica she led Mariam towards the car park. Mariam turned round and waved at Zaiba one last time, her face the happiest she'd ever seen it. Zaiba blinked back in their direction. Had her arch nemesis actually become her *friend*?

"One thing's for sure, if she's going to join us again, she has to get more sensible shoes," Poppy said looking over Zaiba's shoulder.

"We did it, Pops! We're even better detectives than

before. Now we have two solved cases under our belts. Aunt Fouzia will be delighted!"

"She is!" Sam said sneaking up behind Zaiba. She pulled out her phone and there on video chat was Aunt Fouzia's face: big, round and smiling!

"Well done, Beti, you solved your second crime! I am *so* proud."

"But Aunt Fouzia, the detective trail didn't go to plan." Zaiba still felt guilty that the last clue had been tampered with.

"Oh, nonsense." Aunt Fouzia waved her hand. "You showed those children how to solve a *real* crime. That's even better! And you make an excellent snow leopard!"

Suddenly, Zaiba caught the glint of something gold and shiny piled behind her auntie in the background.

"Aunt Fouzia, where are you?" Zaiba asked carefully.

Aunt Fouzia moved the camera close to her face and whispered, "I can't say." She tapped her nose. "But a certain Bollywood star is going to be very happy to get this back!"

The gold stolen from the bank vault! Before Zaiba

could ask anything more, the screen went black. She beamed. The Snow Leopard Detective Agency had solved two crimes that day!

"Hey, how about a group selfie?" Hassan called, pulling Ali and Zaiba up next to him. Poppy held on to Jessica's hand and they all squashed together.

"What shall we say instead of cheese?" Sam asked.

Zaiba grinned. "I know. *Cake!*"

As the family gathered to inspect the photo, Zaiba noticed a small group of her detective-trail contestants standing nervously nearby. A little boy stood at the front of the group, clutching a small, brown-paper parcel.

"Hi, Zaiba, we wanted to say ... we're sorry the detective trail didn't end how you wanted it to."

"Your trail was the most fun we've had at the summer fete, ever!" his older brother said enthusiastically. The rest of the group nodded.

Zaiba felt her tummy go giddy but in a nice way. Her trail *had* been a success after all, and she'd managed to train up some potential new recruits. Aunt Fouzia's legacy was going to be safe in her hands.

"We all put our pocket money together and bought you this present from the book stand to say thank you." The little boy offered over the brown-paper parcel.

"Wow, thank you!" Zaiba was astonished. What on earth could they have found for her?

As she unwrapped the paper, she couldn't believe her eyes. She opened the front page and realized she was looking at the only Eden Lockett novel she didn't own, and the title couldn't have been more perfect: *P Is for Poison!*

"Quick! Let me get an official photo!" Ali ran over with his camera and the new detectives gathered around Zaiba and Poppy. Zaiba held out her new Eden Lockett book in pride of place.

"Three cheers for the Snow Leopard Detective Agency!" cried one of the girls.

"Snow Leopard Detective Agency – UK branch!" Zaiba reminded her. They all cheered again, though even Zaiba had to admit that was quite a mouthful. But as her brother snapped away with his camera, she couldn't help beaming with pride.

With the help of her best friend, her brother and cousin, she'd cracked another case – as well as organizing a successful detective trail. This was certain to make its way into the school newspaper!

"Come on, everyone. Time to say goodbye," said Zaiba's mum. Zaiba high-fived her teams of detectives as they all went back to their own parents. Zaiba, Poppy and Ali went to join their mum and dad, who were standing with Poppy's mum.

"How was the dog show?" Poppy asked as they joined the grown-ups.

Her mum pulled a face. "Nerves got the better of a Pomeranian," she said, "and he had an, ahem, accident at the start line. One little boy burst out crying."

"Oh dear." Zaiba laughed. She could tell Ali was getting ready to make a joke and she gave him a warning look – but it was too late.

"A pooping Poo-meranian!" he cried. "That dog should have won first prize."

The parents shook their heads and Poppy's mum led her away, the two of them waving goodbye.

It had been the perfect summer fete – give or take the odd poisoning. As Zaiba and the others turned to walk home across the village green, she glanced back at the school one last time. Ms Goremain was standing at the gates, smiling. The Lady Mayor was wandering back towards the caretaker's house, holding hands with Peter – his roses had worked! Even Mr Hanlon was looking pleased as he oversaw the taking down of the tents and stands. And Marco was strolling home with Gabriele, the two of them chatting animatedly.

Being a good detective wasn't simply about solving crimes – it was about restoring peace and harmony. And Zaiba had done that, not just for the school but also for the entire village.

Of course, I didn't do it alone, she thought, passing the rhododendron flowers one last time. *I needed my friends*.

That was the most important thing she'd learned today. A good detective was nothing without her friends and family.

She shrugged her yellow bag off her shoulders and

slipped *P Is for Poison* inside with the other books. One of them fell open where the spine was cracked and she glimpsed a final note from her ammi that couldn't have been more perfect for the day:

Even in the sleepiest of towns, mystery is just around the corner!

Zaiba smiled. It certainly was.

DO YOU HAVE WHAT IT TAKES
TO JOIN ZAIBA AND THE SNOW
LEOPARD DETECTIVE AGENCY?

TURN THE PAGE
TO FIND OUT!

THE FLOWER SHOW FELONY
BY EDEN LOCKETT

EXCLUSIVE EXTRACT

That smell! So sweet, so familiar...

"Are you quite all right, Miss Lockett?" Mrs Grainger peered at me in concern, a scone frozen halfway to her lips.

My furrowed brow must have given me away! *Remain calm, Eden,* I told myself. *Don't let your face reveal your deductions.*

"Yes, thank you," I said, flashing her my best smile.

The man sitting on the other side of me huffed yet again. "What's taking those policemen so long?"

"I'm sure we'll be questioned soon, Mr Steele," I said soothingly.

Miss Underwood, the only other person at the table, groaned dramatically. "Ooh, what if they arrest ME!"

"Why would they? It wasn't you who tried to sabotage Mr Alsop's garden," Mrs Grainger said, reaching for another scone. "Or was it?"

Miss Underwood yelped. "Of course not! Poor man! And how CAN you think of food at a time like this?"

Mrs Grainger's only reply was to spoon more jam on to her scone. Jam before cream – scandalous!

I leaned back in my chair and tried to peek through the tent flap, hoping to get a glimpse of the gazebo next door where Inspector Withers was conducting his interviews. But a police constable was standing outside, blocking my view.

I let my chair's two front legs plop back down to the ground and glanced round the table. Myself, Mrs Grainger, Miss Underwood and Mr Steele. Hmmm. We were the only four visitors at the Featherdale Flower Show still to be summoned for questioning.

I knew that I wasn't the saboteur. I wasn't even supposed to be detecting – I had planned a relaxing day off at the flower show! But I was almost certain that the perpetrator was sitting at this table.

My detective nostrils flared again. That sweet scent in the air – it could only be honeysuckle! I knew from my observations that there was only one garden exhibit including this plant – Mr Alsop's. I'd noticed it earlier while sneakily peering round the constable guarding the crime scene (honestly, why *do* the police insist on getting in the way?).

I thought back to my discreet questioning of the three people at the table. All of them had claimed they'd never gone near Mr Alsop's garden. So where was the honeysuckle smell coming from? Even the best detective can't go around sniffing suspects.

That's when I spotted Mrs Grainger's flowery summer jacket slung on the back of her chair.

I gave a theatrical shiver and rubbed my bare arms. "Oh, it's getting a bit chilly, isn't it?"

Mrs Grainger swivelled round slightly to grab her jacket. "Here you go, Miss Lockett. You can borrow this."

"So kind," I murmured, slipping it round my

shoulders and taking a deep sniff. Honeysuckle. Strong, sweet, unmistakable honeysuckle.

"Your jacket has such a lovely smell!" I said. "Just like honeysuckle. Your perfume, I suppose?"

Mrs Grainger snorted. "I can't stand honeysuckle. I won't even have any in my garden – I certainly wouldn't have perfume scented with the stuff!"

I looked her straight in the eye. "Well then, I suppose it must have brushed off on to your jacket when you were in Mr Alsop's garden exhibit ... when you were trying to sabotage his display?"

Mrs Grainger turned the colour of the jam she was busy spreading on another scone. "How dare—"

But it was too late for her to deny my accusations. The blush travelling up her throat gave her away.

No criminal can argue with Eden Locket's detective nose!

AMMI'S ADVICE

Zaiba's ammi gives the best advice. Here are some of her top tips to keep in mind during an investigation!

🔍 If plan A doesn't work, there's a whole alphabet worth of letters left to try!

🔍 Don't just question what HAS happened, question what HASN'T happened. You have to question EVERYTHING.

🔍 The most exciting mysteries are the ones left unsolved!

🔍 Maybe solving a crime is like walking in a maze!

🔍 Even in the sleepiest of towns, mystery is just around the corner!

PLAN YOUR OWN DETECTIVE TRAIL

Zaiba's detective trail was the most popular activity at the school fete. Why not create your own exciting trail? You can make it as big or small as you want, but these things might be useful:

🔍 Pen and paper to record findings

🔍 A range of clues

🔍 Disguises

🔍 Character information sheets (you could ask friends or family to play different roles in the investigation)

🔍 Suggested questions for your detectives

The key to a detective trail is the crime! Once you've decided what it is going to be, you need to know who the victim and criminal are, where it took place and what weapon was used or item was stolen.

Now *you* know what happened, it's time to let the others work it out! There are different ways you can point your budding detectives to the answer:

PHYSICAL ITEMS such as letters, notes or tickets can be left for investigators to find. Mentions of places, people or events that sound suspicious could lead the detective to the scene of the crime, location of the hidden item or introduce a new suspect...

CONVERSATIONS can reveal secrets or motives. If you have friends helping, the detectives could overhear useful information or interrogate suspects. If you decide not to use actors, the detectives could hear a voice mail. Your character sheets and prompts will make sure these interactions further the investigation.

PUZZLES can be a fun way to challenge your detectives! Encourage them to solve riddles and crack codes to learn new information.

RED HERRINGS: While you want to guide the detectives towards the answer, you don't want to make it too easy for them. Maybe throw in one or two red herrings – but not too many or it can be frustrating!

EVIDENCE: You'll need to leave enough physical clues to provide the detective with evidence once they've solved the crime – ready for their big reveal!

Now you're all set to create your own mystery. You can even use some of Zaiba's extra helpful notes in this book and *THE MISSING DIAMOND* to help your trainee detectives. And remember – the key element is fun!

Ready, set, DETECT!

TRAIN YOUR BRAIN!

In her detective trail, Zaiba set her aspiring investigators challenges – it's important as a detective to train your brain! Can you solve Zaiba's tricky puzzles?

RIDDLES:

1. What can travel around the world but never leaves the corner?

2. What has to be broken before you can use it?

3. I'm tall when I'm young and short when I'm old – what am I?

4. What is always in front of you but can't be seen?

5. What belongs to you, but other people use it more than you do?

6. Ayisha's parents have three children: Rayan, Sofia and what's the name of the third child?

7. The more you take, the more you leave behind.

Answers: 1. A stamp 2. An egg 3. A candle 4. The future 5. Your name 6. Ayisha 7. Footprints

CODE BREAKERS:

When Zaiba, Mariam and Poppy are locked in the science classroom then try to use Morse Code to get help. Using the grid below, can you tell what these messages say?

1. -.. --- -. -   . .- -   - .... .   -.-. .- -.- .

2. .-.. --- --- -.-   --- ...- . .-   - .... . .-. .

3. .... . .-.. .-.. ---   -.. . - . -.-. - .. ...- .

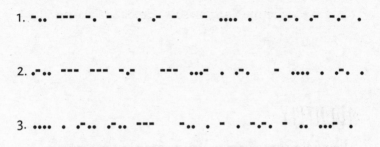

A	● ▬	N	▬ ●
B	▬ ● ● ●	O	▬ ▬ ▬
C	▬ ● ▬ ●	P	● ▬ ▬ ●
D	▬ ● ●	Q	▬ ▬ ● ▬
E	●	R	● ▬ ●
F	● ● ▬ ●	S	● ● ●
G	▬ ▬ ●	T	▬
H	● ● ● ●	U	● ● ▬
I	● ●	V	● ● ● ▬
J	● ▬ ▬ ▬	W	● ▬ ▬
K	▬ ● ▬	X	▬ ● ● ▬
L	● ▬ ● ●	Y	▬ ● ▬ ▬
M	▬ ▬	Z	▬ ▬ ● ●

SURPRISE DISGUISE!

**Being a detective means being ready for anything –
you never know when you might need to go under cover!**

IDENTITY

Depending on your case, you might need to assume a
new role to collect information. Pick a character who
would have reason to be in that particular situation.

If you have time, invent a backstory! Spend time getting
into character to be on top acting form.

You could even try and change your voice and the way
you walk! Subtle changes could make all the difference.

COSTUME

The most important thing about your costume is
that you don't stand out. You want to blend into
the background – so your outfit will depend on the
background!

You can use clothing to change your appearance in
several ways – for example wearing lots of layers to
change your size, as well as removing layers to change
your look.

You could use costume as a distraction – for example
having your face painted as a puffer fish!

Accessories such as hats, sunglasses, scarves, masks and
wigs will make you harder to recognise.

Over to you, agents! See you out there ...
or maybe not!

CAKES!

Make Hassan's prize winning
Cardamom and Lemon Loaf Cake!

Remember to make sure you've asked an adult's permission before you start baking, and ask for help when using the oven. Happy baking!

Ingredients

- Butter, softened 170g
- Self raising flour 170g
- Light brown sugar 170g
- 3 eggs
- Juice and zest of 2 large lemons
- 2 teaspoons of ground cardamom, (you can also buy green cardamom pods, scrape out the seeds from inside and grind them up yourself)
- 1 teaspoon baking powder
- Icing sugar to decorate

Method

1. Preheat oven to 180c / Gas Mark 4.

2. Grease a loaf tin and line it with non-stick baking paper.

3. In a mixing bowl, sift in your flour and baking powder. Then add the butter, sugar, lemon zest and cardamom. Beat it all together until it's fluffy and light in colour.

4. Slowly add in the eggs a little at a time, beating the mixture as you go. If the mixture starts to curdle (gets thick and lumpy) then add in a little flour until it combines together.

5. Mix in half the lemon juice. Then transfer mixture to loaf tin.

6. Bake the loaf for 35 minutes, until it's golden on top and cooked all the way through the middle. You can stick a fork in and if it comes out clean, you know your sponge is cooked.

7. Prick holes in the top of the warm sponge and pour the remaining lemon juice evenly over the sponge.

8. Wait for the sponge to cool completely before removing it from the tin.

9. You can dust the top of the sponge with icing sugar, or slices of lemon. Get creative and decorate!

10. Enjoy your yummy cake!

ACKNOWLEDGEMENTS

I would like to give a huge thank you to my agent Davinia Andrew-Lynch and to Karen Ball at Speckled Pen. You two have truly been the most supportive and encouraging friends and mentors to me. Thank you for believing in me and bringing Agent Zaiba to life.

Also to everyone at Stripes, I couldn't have asked for a lovelier publishing team for my first books. Thank you for your genuine enthusiasm and care. A special thank you to Daniela for creating such gorgeous illustrations of Zaiba and her world.

Finally, thank you to my family and friends, always.

– Annabelle Sami

ABOUT THE AUTHOR

Annabelle Sami is a writer and performer.
She grew up next to the sea on the south coast of the
UK and moved to London, where she now lives, for
university. At Queen Mary University she had an amazing
time studying English Literature and Drama, finally
graduating with an MA in English Literature.

When she isn't writing she enjoys playing saxophone
in a band with her friends, performing live art
and swimming in the sea!

ABOUT THE ILLUSTRATOR

Originally from Romania, Daniela Sosa now lives and works in Cambridge with her husband and is completing an MA in children's book illustration at the Cambridge School of Art.

Creating a magical mix of the ordinary and the unusual, Daniela enjoys highlighting subtle detail and finding beauty in everyday life. She gets inspiration from nature, books and observing the world around.

HELP ZAIBA SOLVE HER NEXT CRIME IN...

Agent Zaiba
INVESTIGATES

THE HAUNTED HOUSE